ABOUT THE AU

George G. Gilman was born in 1936 in what was then a small village east of London. He attended local schools until the age of fifteen. Upon leaving school he abandoned all earlier ambitions and decided to become a professional writer, with strong leanings towards the mystery novel. He wrote short stories and books during evenings, lunch hours, at weekends, and on the time of various employers while he worked for an international newsagency, a film company, a weekly book-trade magazine and the Royal Air Force.

His first short (love) story was published when he was sixteen and the first (mystery) novel ten years later. He has been a full-time writer since 1970, writing mostly Westerns which have been translated into a dozen languages and have sold in excess of 16 million copies. He is married and lives on the Dorset coast, which is as far west as he intends to move right now.

THE LONG SHADOW

George G. Gilman

NEW ENGLISH LIBRARY
Hodder and Stoughton

for
Kitty and, of
course, Ben.

Copyright © 1989 by
George G. Gilman

First published in Great Britain
in 1989 by New English Library
paperbacks

An NEL paperback original

British Library C.I.P.

Gilman, George G. *1936–*
   The long shadow.
   Rn. Terry Harknett
   I. Title
   823'.914[F]

ISBN 0-450-49730-5

Printed and bound in Great
Britain for Hodder and Stoughton
paperbacks, a division of Hodder
and Stoughton Ltd., Mill Road,
Dunton Green, Sevenoaks, Kent
TN13 2YA (Editorial Office: 47
Bedford Square, London, WC1B
3DP) by Cox & Wyman Ltd.,
Reading, Berks.

1

About all Al Strachen knew of horses was how to ride them—and that you fed them at the front and whenever possible it was wise to stay clear of the rear. But there was a lot more to running a stud ranch than knowing a whole lot about horses. And Strachen possessed a powerful frame along with an eager willingness to work his muscles hard on any kind of chore that did not call for special skills.

So it did not take long for Adam Steele to realise he had made a wise move hiring on Strachen to help out with the summer work that needed to be done on the three and a half thousand acre spread known as Trail's End.

This reflection, which brought a quiet smile of satisfaction to his bearded face as he leaned his back against the hitching rail out front of the Golden Gate, a cup of coffee grasped in one gloved hand, was triggered by the way another hired-on worker was getting noisily and irritatingly drunk in the saloon. The kind of drunk, Steele had figured, who would be spoiling for a fight right after he took one drink too many: which always might be the next one.

Usually the Virginian sat inside Harry Krim's place to drink a cup of the saloonkeeper's good coffee while he waited for his orders for supplies to be made up in the stores across the square of downtown Providence. Passing the time of day with Krim, or the likes of Doc Mackay, Roland Decker, Harlan Grout or Tom Knight: or any out-of-town farmer or rancher who happened to be taking a drink in the saloon that morning.

In fact, the men whose names came to mind were all in the Golden Gate right now: the core of the saloon's regular patrons, known for their liking of beer and liquor. But this morning the place was a lot more crowded than usual, the customary group of regulars augmented by more than the average number of people from places to the north and south along the Providence River Valley, and the town in the timber. Likewise, the stores in back of the roofed sidewalk along the western side of the square were doing better than usual Friday morning business.

For this was the last Friday of the month and on this day each four or five weeks a Concord coach of the San Francisco and Central California Stage Line Company came to Providence. Which was considered an event of interest by a large number of people in this isolated community where they led such restricted lives, usually starved of incident.

When Steele set out aboard his flatbed wagon to drive from the spread to town, a half mile down the Timber Creek spur and another half mile along the main trail from Broadwater, it had not registered in his mind that today the stage was due in. But it made little difference to him, except that the saloon and the stores were more crowded than usual at mid-morning: with people waiting eagerly for mail or goods, to see an infrequent stranger to town, maybe, or hear word-of-mouth news from the driver and shotgun.

Maybe, Steele reflected idly as he shifted his back into a more comfortable position against the hitching rail, it was not such a well attended event as it used to be since the telegraph line had been extended the ten miles from Broadwater into Providence. Now Huey Attrill made extensive use of the wire to obtain news of the outside world for the weekly *Providence Post-Despatch*.

But it still caused the saloon to be overcrowded, which was fine for Harry Krim's cash drawer, but not for Steele who disliked crowded places. Neither did the Virginian enjoy the company of men who drank but could not hold their liquor. And Nick Deeker, the young man Abe Steiner had hired on to help with the summer work at Mission Farm, was running short of willing listeners for his loud talk on any unrelated subject that came to mind—was working his way round to close in on the table where Steele sat when the Virginian decided to move outside and drink his cup of coffee. While he waited for Harold Archer to make up his grocery order, Matthew Cody to get ready some sacks of feed and Amelia Decker to supply the cuts he had asked for at the meat market.

Soon, though, he was grateful to the raucous Decker who

was building up to becoming an obnoxious drunk. For he quickly discovered it was no hardship to be out on the square with buildings on three sides and timber to the south this sunlit, warm, California June morning. Hearing the kids in Lavinia Attwood's school as they sang, albeit not too tunefully, about how the world was so bright and beautiful because that was how God had made it and meant it to be.

It surely was bright and beautiful for him now that he had become an accepted member of this community in the timbered valley cutting through the western foothills of the Sierra Nevadas of central California: had established himself securely on those three and a half thousand acres of prime grazing land where others had once attempted, long ago, to put down roots, and failed.

Was successful enough to afford to hire some help at the going rate without feeling any pinch. And along with success, his luck was seemingly still holding: the way he had taken on a man of the calibre of Al Strachen instead of one like Nick Deeker!

Fate had arbitrarily steered him to the derelict house and abandoned acres and he had to allow he had used up more than his fair share of good luck in getting the place into shape. But pure and simple good fortune would have been useless without the tenacity he applied to making a success of Trail's End.

The kind of violent trouble that had dogged him throughout his life as a drifter was not ended when he made the decision to call a halt, put down roots in a place where he could recreate something close to his lost birthright. And for a while—quite a time—local people had considered the violence to be his fault, so there had been much hostility stirred up toward him.

But among a growing number of people, the way he took such a firm line in handling the trouble led to an acceptance that without him Providence would have fared much worse. And gradually the vast majority of townspeople along with those on the scattered places up and down the river valley began to regard Adam Steele as a welcome newcomer to this piece of California.

And not for something like a year now had any trouble of a violent nature happened here in town or out at Trail's End.

There had been an explosion of violence and death in which

he felt compelled to take a hand earlier this year. An incident which involved a coach of the SF&CC stage line, he reflected with a scowl as he heard the distant sounds of the Concord and six-horse team approaching town on the north trail. But that had happened far away, when he was returning home from a business trip to San Francisco.

And, anyway, like all the rest of the trouble which had struck closer to home, that was water under the bridge, he told himself as his face lost the scowl and took on its usual impassive set behind and above the beard. This as the clatter of the Concord's approach began to drown out the less than melodious singing of the schoolchildren. Became loud enough to reach inside the buildings on three sides of the square, draw out from some of them those people who made a point of being in town for the arrival of the stage. And others who had business connected with the stage.

This latter group included Harlan Grout, the thirty year old liveryman, stockily built and running to fat, who drank too much but seldom enough to get drunk. He emerged from the saloon, headed for his stable up beyond the stage line depot and the bank, hopeful of making a little extra drinking money out of tending to any team horse that had need of his undoubted skills as a liveryman or as an unqualified but reasonably competent vetinerary.

The twenty years older, narrow-chested and pot-bellied Tom Knight, who ran Grout a close second for the title of hardest drinker in Providence, also came out from the batwinged entrance of the saloon and hurried to the boarding house on the other side of the livery from the bank. Got there just as his short and grossly overweight wife stepped on to the porch under the ROOMS FOR RENT sign, glared her disapproval of where he had been, then peered toward the end of the north trail between the law office and the meeting hall. The Knights always hoped to see passengers step off the stage: strangers to town, needing board and lodging in their establishment, renowned for its cleanliness and the fine food Blanche cooked and served.

Sheriff Len Fallows, who was fifty two, tall and lean, with a rough-hewn, sun-burnished face dominated by a black moustache, was as neatly attired as his wife always ensured when he stepped out of his office and started toward the stage line depot. He was as impassive-faced as Steele as he advanced officiously through the morning sunlight, a Frontier Colt in a tied down holster: the only man on the square to tote a gun. But he did so as nothing more than an adjunct to the badge of office pinned to the left side of his shirt front. For Fallows had no cause to expect trouble to ride in on the stage, but as local peace officer he felt it was his duty to be in close touch with all that went on in his jurisdiction.

'Mr Steele,' he greeted curtly as he angled across the corner formed by the saloon and the stage line depot, then tipped his hat to the skinny, angular-featured Jeanne Morrison who had run the depot and telegraph office single handed for most of the time since her bachelor son was murdered in the schoolyard last year.

Almost a year ago, Steele realised as he nodded to acknowledge Fallows' greeting, then tipped his own hat to Mrs Morrison. For it was June now and it was on the night of the Independence Day social last year when Michael was stabbed to death.

Ethan Brady hurried out of his bank and toward Mrs Morrison, who smiled her relief that the sixty years old, short and flabby, nervously dispositioned man was once more coming to her assistance in time of need.

Several knowing smiles were shown by the crowd gathering out front of the stage line depot as they saw the exchange of looks between the banker and the woman ten years his junior. For it was common knowledge the two had been attracted to each other ever since Mrs Morrison was widowed—some said even before this long ago event—and only the disapproval of the woman's son had prevented the two marrying. Since Michael had died and the pain of his loss had been partially healed by the passage of time, most expected it would not be long before the Reverend Joseph Marlow was asked to perform a wedding ceremony.

Then all thoughts unconnected with the here and now were pushed from the minds of the watchers as the stage rolled into sight and the team was steered into a turn that brought the rig toward the north east corner of the square. Where it turned again in front of the saloon, halted before the depot. There was no haste about its arrival and little dust was stirred by the

11

hooves and wheelrims. The coats of the horses were unlathered by sweat and smiles showed on the faces of the elderly driver and the younger man who rode shotgun as they waved and yelled back acknowledgements of the greetings called to them.

Plainly there had been no trouble back up the trail, which had become a cause of relief since the hold-up of a stage on this run not so long ago.

'Somebody real important comin' in on the stage today? The President, maybe, or somebody like that?'

Steele knew who posed the question before he turned and saw Deeker's face above the batwing doors of the saloon. A young face, but already starting to acquire a dissipated look from over-indulgence in hard liquor.

The hand Abe Steiner had hired on was about twenty five with basically handsome features under jet black curly hair. He was fresh-complexioned, with blue eyes and a well-formed mouth that was quick to smile: but with a brand of humour always tinged with cynicism that struck a wrong note in one of his few years. He had a strong looking frame, almost six feet tall, on which his drinking had not yet had visible effect.

Steele had only seen Deeker for the first time this morning, but had already formed an opinion of him that was not based entirely upon the fact he was a drinker who could not hold his drink. For ever since the Virginian had settled at Trail's End and only infrequently came into contact with strangers, he considered he had developed a reliable ability to make a sound judgment of character on the shortest of acquaintance.

Or maybe, he briefly thought, he had simply become as restricted in his view of his fellow human kind as were most of the people he now lived among. Looked for the most obvious faults in a stranger and made his assessment from them.

'I don't know,' he told the flush-faced man, bloodshot-eyed and slurred of voice, whose expression formed into a disdainful sneer as he watched the people close in on the stage and team as soon as the Concord came to a standstill.

'Some folks around here just like to come see the stage roll in, Mr Deeker,' Harry Krim explained as he moved up behind the drunk in the saloon entrance.

The red-haired, broad-shouldered saloonkeeper, pot-bellied and some forty years old, was as interested as any local citizen to see if anybody got off the stage: hopeful it would be a stranger in need of a drink or two. But in his eyes now there was a kind of sheepishness as he briefly met the gaze of Steele. An acceptance of the censure that may have been in back of the Virginian's impassiveness: criticism of a man who had sold another more than enough liquor for his own good.

And the good of Krim himself, who tried to keep trouble out of the Golden Gate, but on occasion allowed his greed for gain to overrule his good sense based upon the experience of seeing too many men drink too much and cause trouble.

Did he hold such an opinion, Steele asked himself? He had moved out of the saloon on account of the drunken young man. Was this another sign of his mind getting narrower as he settled deeper into the new way of life?

'Well,' Deeker growled, and the sneer in his voice matched the look on his face as he pushed out between the batwings with a swaggering gait. 'I guess that's about what's to be expected in a hick town like this. Where about the only thing to get excited about is the sun comin' up every mornin', then settin' each night.'

Steele needed to make a conscious effort not to regard the drunk's remark as a personal slight against him.

Krim moved up to the batwings, hooked his hands over them to stop them swinging.

Roland Decker called from where he sat at the rear of the bar room: 'Way local folks like the town to be, son! Nobody's forced to stay here if they don't want to.'

'Unless they break the law and they have to spend time in the lock-up.'

This was growled by Len Fallows who stood at the rear of the crowd, closer to the saloon than the newly arrived stage, off which the driver and guard were climbing. The sheriff turned to glare at Deeker, in time to see him bang painfully into the end of the hitching rail and vent a low curse.

'It breakin' the law for a man to take a drink?' Deeker challenged sourly as he rubbed his belly where the rail had dug into him.

'Getting drunk and bothering other people is,' Fallows warned coldly.

Deeker came to a halt and exclaimed: 'Wow!'

13

But he was not responding to what Fallows told him. He was looking, together with almost everyone else, toward a woman stepping down from the stage. A woman of the kind likely to trigger such an exclamation in the mind if not to the lips of any red-blooded man who saw her for the first time.

And maybe some others did utter this or a similar sound at about the same time as Nick Deeker, for there was a quality of admiration mixed with lust in the brief buzz of noise that heralded a briefer silence. Before the beaming young shotgun rider who was helping the woman out of the Concord announced:

'This here is Mrs Ruth Blair. Come all the way from Denver. By way of San Francisco, right ma'am?'

'I sure would enjoy havin' her go all the way with me,' Nick Deeker said huskily. And maybe more loudly than he had intended.

As with the exclamation, probably every man who looked at Ruth Blair thought what Deeker had spoken. For she was a stunningly attractive woman. Tall and fine figured. With blonde hair that tumbled to her shoulders in highly sheened waves at either side of her classically-boned, full-lipped, large-eyed face.

Her luxuriant hair cascaded from under a small black hat, a colour matched by a mourning band around her left upper arm. The rest of her outfit was comprised of a white blouse, pale blue jacket and long, flared skirt.

Steele thought she was on the wrong side of thirty, maybe closer to forty. Which she attempted to conceal with paint and powder. Freshly and skilfully applied far down the ten miles of trail from Broadwater, so she would be seen at her best when she stepped off the stage in Providence.

Which she did with an almost regal air: like she was familiar with making an entrance, confidently expected the admiring reception she invariably received in these circumstances.

She had shown a gentle smile tinged with sadness before she heard what Nick Deeker said, and swung her head to glower at him with a withering mixture of disdain and indignant anger.

Then Steele saw her express shock before he shifted his attention from her, toward the sudden flurry of activity that caused the change in the woman.

Len Fallows had whirled and now he lunged toward the lecherously-grinning Deeker. Whose reflexes were slowed by a combination of the liquor that dulled his brain and his lustful preoccupation with the beautiful blonde frozen in the act of descending from the stage.

He may have been aware at the last moment of something rushing toward his head. But probably he did not register what this was until the fist of the Providence lawman slammed viciously into his face. And he yelled, was driven by the force of the powerful impact into a clumsy backward run for a few steps. Before he tripped over his own feet and fell down hard. Suffered more pain as the back of his head crashed into the rock-hard ground of the square.

'Shit!' he snarled through teeth gritted between curled back lips.

'Insulting a lady doesn't sit well with Providence folks!' Len Fallows rasped.

Ethan Brady encouraged: 'Hear, hear!'

This drew other words of agreement from men and women clustered around the stage.

'Nor does cussing in the hearing of women!' Roland Decker called from within the saloon.

But Fallows was not prepared to take the situation any further unless he had to. And he turned away as Nick Deeker folded up gingerly into a sitting posture and the more mundane sounds and activity connected with the arrival of the stage re-started.

Thus, when Deeker glowered around as he started to struggle to his feet, he saw that few people paid him any attention. And of those that did, only Adam Steele eyed him with anything less than undisguised contempt. For the Virginian looked at him impassively, which could have been construed as a mask for any emotion.

'What the hell did I say?' the young drunk who had sobered up asked sourly.

'You insulted a lady,' Harry Krim supplied, recalled he was addressing a good customer and added: 'Mr Deeker.'

Deeker shook his fuzzed head, scowled as he complained: 'As I recall, I only meant to say what a beauty she is.'

He groaned as he attained to his feet and straightened up.

15

Swayed a little as he massaged the small of his back with one hand, the back of his head with the other. Then became aware that the source of his greatest discomfort was the point where Len Fallows' fist had connected.

Before he covered his left eye with a cupped hand, Steele glimpsed the start of the swelling and discoloration at the top of the cheek and the brow above.

'Nobody can argue with that, can they?' Deeker asked as he shifted his attention back to the new arrival in Providence. 'She is one fine lookin' woman, ain't she?'

'Reckon so,' Steele allowed pensively. 'In your case, a sight for a sore eye.'

2

Steele took a few seconds to finish his cooled coffee, and returned the empty cup to Harry Krim. Then he moved without haste across the square and collected his made up orders from the grocery, the meat market and the feed and seed store. Loaded his purchases on to the rear of the flatbed and was ready to leave town on the north trail ahead of the stage, which no longer was a focus of eager attention.

Without asking questions or purposely eavesdropping on several conversations, he acquired several items of news and overheard a quantity of gossip related to the arrival of the stage and its striking-looking passenger.

She was a widow of several months and it was a matter of conjecture among some of the townswomen whether the sombre hue of her hat was intended as a sign of mourning or merely to fashionably complement the black armband. Mrs Blair was going to take a room at the Knight boarding house. Nobody had so far managed to learn the reason for her visit to Providence.

The elderly driver of the stage and his young shotgun rider had nothing of importance or vicarious interest to report about happenings in San Francisco or any of the stopover towns between the distant city and Providence that had not already been printed in the columns of Huey Attrill's newspaper.

If anybody had received noteworthy news in a letter or anything of general interest in a package carried over many miles in the forward or rear boots of the Concord coach, they were not yet ready to make it public.

Lack of news travelled as fast as a plethora of it in Providence.

Steele heard a woman in the grocery store voice the

17

disdainfully-toned opinion that widow Mrs Ruth Blair might well be, but she looked like she was no better than she ought to be and Len Fallows would do well to keep a close watch on what she got up to.

The sixty-years-old, squint-eyed and sightly lame Harold Archer harshly rebuked his customer for expressing this sentiment and warned her it was only because she was a woman that he did not respond to what she said in the same way the sheriff had countered Deeker's insult.

The woman, from one of the out-of-town farmsteads, moved across the threshold of the grocery on to the sidewalk before she sneered that it was only to be expected that a man would be infatuated with that kind of loose-looking woman and come to her defence.

Steele found himself agreeing first with the less attractive, older than Ruth Blair farmer's wife. Then with Harold Archer. And again with the woman. But once he was aboard the flatbed and had steered the horse in the traces into a tight turn away from the line of stores behind the roofed sidewalk, he attempted to forget everything concerned with the arrival of the stage and its passenger.

Relished the prospect of returning to Trail's End, where there would no longer be need to examine his responses to anything that was no business of his: to discover whether his feelings were justified or not. If they were good or bad in the circumstances: better based now on a more worthy set of premises than they would have been when he was a drifting saddletramp.

At the spread he would only have the company of Al Strachen, who managed to combine a friendly disposition with a liking for lengthy silences that Steele found as much a quality of the man as his ability to work long and hard without supervision.

As he drove the flatbed toward the beginning of the north trail, he took the time to tip his hat to Lavinia Attwood as she emerged from the arched doorway of the schoolhouse, started to shepherd her students outside for the noon hour break. And as had happened for some time now, the fifty-five-years-old spinster, tall and skinny, sharp-featured, bespectacled and grey-haired, responded to his polite greeting with a warm smile and a friendly wave which did not conceal any deeper feelings. Gone, thankfully, were the days when the schoolma'am had romantic inclinations toward him.

On the other side of the square, the two-man crew had left the area where the stage stood, after conferring with Harlan Grout and deciding the team horses needed no attention. Were doubtless in the Golden Gate, sinking a beer or two to lay the dust while they engaged in man talk with the other customers.

Which was what usually happened on the last Friday of each month when the SF&CC Concord reached the end of its southbound run. Soon it would head back to Broadwater, the older and larger town, which was by custom the place where the team was changed and the crew overnighted.

With no pressing need to make fast time, and easily able to keep his mind free of disturbing lines of thought as he reflected on how bright and beautiful his world was, it took Steele maybe fifteen minutes to reach the point where Timber Creek joined the broader Providence River and the spur to Trail's End forked off to the west and forded the river.

The horse made known his need of a drink from the clear, slow-flowing water and Steele was not hard put to sit on the unmoving rig, listening to the trickling sounds of the river and creek, the bird songs in the surrounding timber: smelling the clean, fresh scents of water and trees heavy with summer leaf. Thinking about what awaited him at the end of the spur that followed the creek.

The kind of place that as a young man, son of one of the wealthiest plantation owners in Virginia, would have seemed like nothing at all in his estimation.

Then, for many violent years after the War Between the States robbed him of his rich birthright and he drifted wherever fate took him, the kind of place that would have held no appeal for him.

But today, more than four years after he took the resolute decision to put down his roots, he was prepared to defend the spread to the death.

Even if it lacked one important component, damnit!

He was not often aware of what was missing from Trail's

End, but when he was made aware of it—during long, lonesome nights or when the sight of a beautiful woman made the lack so clear—there was an ache triggered so deep inside him he was prepared to admit to himself he possessed something he generally considered he had been born without.

A soul, Goddamnit!

But just because he had this morning seen such a woman who had struck a chord deep in his soul, and he was ready to feel as badly toward Len Fallows for beating him to the punch with Nick Deeker as he did toward the hired hand for insulting Ruth Blair, that didn't have to mean . . .

He heard a series of sounds similar to that which had interrupted his train of thought when he was taking his ease against the Golden Gate hitching rail, reflecting on how fine was his world: irrespective of the fact that a woman did not figure in it.

And now he turned on the seat of the wagon to look south down the trail. Where the six horse team hauled the stage into sight around a curve out of the timber, rolled along one of the few stretches of trail between Providence and Broadwater where it and the river ran parallel with each other for a short way.

The crew saw the wagon stalled in the river and the young, freckle-faced, suspicious-eyed shotgun rider was suddenly nervous, fisted a hand around the rifle rested across his lap when the grey-haired, leather-skinned driver said something to him. A few moments later, while Steele stayed unmoving on the seat and the shotgun rider remained apprehensive about what was happening, the driver hauled on the reins. Brought the Concord to a gentle stop behind the flatbed, still axle deep in the ford long after the horse had finished drinking from the trickling water that sparkled in the early afternoon sunshine.

'Do something for you fellers?' Steele asked.

The young man looked at the older one, who was peering down at the reins in his hands. Then the driver applied the brake lever, lifted his head to look directly at the Virginian, swallowed hard and said:

'I hear you're Adam Steele?'

'You heard the truth,' the Virginian told him, hid his

concern at the grim expression that came to the older man's face, the way the younger one still nervously clutched the Winchester across his thighs.

Awhile ago, Steele constantly had his own rifle near to hand but nowadays he was often without it close by. Today, it was under the wagon seat, beyond easy reach should the situation turn ugly.

'I reckon a lawman should only tell the truth, Mr Steele. He told me you were the guy ridin' the stage out of Frisco when Ezra and Steve got killed. Back in the springtime?'

'I was a passenger,' Steele confirmed, still unable to read precisely what was behind the harder set expression on the old man's darkly sun-burnished and deeply lined face. It could be hatred or contempt, directed at him or a third, absent party.

The driver grunted. 'I'm Jed Niven. Knew Ezra Royce and Steve Eastman real well. Worked with them a long time. Bill Bundy here, he's Steve's replacement. Never knew either of them.'

Steele said with a pointed look at Bundy: 'I was riding inside when the shootings happened. But I reckon it was Eastman who got trigger happy, tried to be a hero. I don't think the driver wanted him to try anything like that.'

Niven nodded and got a nostalgic look in his eyes when he reached out to the side, laid a hand on the wrist of the hand grasping the rifle. Then assured: 'I don't want no trouble. And there's no call for any, I reckon. Take it easy, Bill. I just wanna satisfy my curiosity.'

He sensed the younger man was still tense, reluctant to relax his state of nervous readiness while he continued to mistrust Steele's impassivity and his partner's line of questioning. Then Niven tightened his grip around Bundy's wrist as he said:

'Steve always was the hasty one in that partnership. There ain't no need for anyone to be hasty here.'

Bundy remained rigid for a moment more, then shrugged and allowed the tension to drain out of his body. Left the rifle resting across his lap as he released it and in turn had his wrist set free by Niven. He dug the makings from a shirt pocket.

Niven also seemed easier in his body and his mind and then

a kind of beseeching look showed in his eyes as he said: 'How they died ain't what I want to hear about, Mr Steele.'

The Virginian inclined his head in a tacit invitation for Niven to take his inquiries further.

'Heard from the sheriff of Bending you went off into the mountains on the track of the men and women who held up the stage. He got told that by the other passengers. Them you left to bring the stage into Bending with the corpses of Ezra and Steve?'

'There's another lawman tells it like it is, feller,' Steele confirmed.

'You caught up with them, he said?'

'I caught up with them.'

'And let them go after you got back what was took from you?'

Steele stooped on the seat and reached under it without hurry. Gripped the Colt Hartford by the muzzle end of the barrel and brought it up into view.

Bundy froze in the process of tipping tobacco from his poke into a strip of paper. But became less tense again when he saw Steele rest the rosewood stock on the seat at his side, still retaining the single-handed grip around the barrel close to the muzzle.

'It's a Colt Hartford, revolver action sporting rifle,' Steele said. 'A family heirloom that's important to me. When anybody lays a hand on it with the intention of stealing it, it seems like it gets to be the most important thing in my life. It's the reason I went after the bunch held up the stage.'

'What I heard.'

'What else do you want to hear?'

Niven took a few moments for thought, like he could not recall the point toward which he was aiming. Or was worried about framing a form of words to ask the question. His gaze kept darting nervously at Steele and away again.

'I've got some time to spare, but——'

'Yeah. Look, how'd it happen you got back your rifle and didn't bring in the bastards killed Ezra and Steve, mister? Specially after one of the other passengers on that stage said he'd give you a thousand bucks for gettin' back his wife's jewels that they stole off her?'

'You accusing me of something?' Steele asked evenly, unable to keep his gloved hand from instinctively tightening its grip around the barrel of the Colt Hartford.

Bundy was feeling the strain again. But although he struck a match on the stock of his Winchester to light the newly rolled cigarette, he did not otherwise touch the rifle.

Niven gave an emphatic shake of his head and waved a hand in a dismissive gesture. Got a sincere look in his eyes as he assured: 'No, no I ain't, mister. They were good buddies of mine. You were there. I just want to know is all. If you don't wanna tell me for some reason, then there's an end to it.'

Steele pursed his lips within his beard for a second or so, then shrugged and nodded. And told Jed Niven about what happened after he rode away from the stage that was so violently held up.

It did not take long, for although the climb up the mountainside had used up many hours, it required no more than a minute to tell of it. And the battle at the abandoned army post in the middle of that cold night could only be strung out into a lengthy tale by someone with a penchant for the dramatic: which Steele did not possess.

Bundy listened with increasing impatience and mounting apprehension, not trusting his partner to accept the unfolding story without a bitter reaction.

And Niven certainly seemed to harden in his attitude as each new fact was revealed. Then, when Steele was through with the telling, he said flatly: 'There was no ammo in the rifle they gave you back, uh?'

'Right.'

'Sure.'

'Lawmen haven't cornered the market in telling the truth, feller.'

Niven was grimly pensive for a moment.

Bundy urged: 'Seems to me you heard what you want to, Jed.'

Steele corrected: 'He heard what I had to tell him, which isn't the same thing.'

The disgruntled older man took up the reins, said: 'Okay. I can understand why you let go them murderin' bastards that didn't get themselves killed in the fight. After you got back

23

what was yours. Didn't try for the thousand bucks you could've earned. Plus a reward from the stage line, maybe.'

'Fine, so let's go,' Bundy pressed.

Niven went on: 'I reckon you did wrong, just lettin' them ride off like that. But I wasn't there, so I can't have no opinion outside of thinkin' you was wrong. Much obliged to you for takin' the time to tell me about it. Specially how it don't show you up in a good light, mister.'

Steele knew the old man wanted to say more on the subject, but was afraid. He asked: 'And I'd be obliged for something from you, feller?'

'What's that?'

'Whatever you can tell me about the woman rode your stage from San Francisco to Providence?'

'Don't know nothin' but her name,' the driver said and reached for the brake lever. 'That and she came from Denver to Frisco. Bought a ticket there to ride to Providence. Plus she's been a widow woman for awhile.'

Now he released the brake blocks off the wheelrims as he spat off the side of the Concord. Fixed Steele with a withering glare as he summoned the courage to add: 'But even if I knew her whole life story, I wouldn't tell it to the kinda selfish sonofabitch that let a bunch of killers get away once he got back off them what they stole off him!'

'Jed!' Bundy growled anxiously and shot a sidelong glance at Steele, as pleading as the look Niven had shown earlier. 'You said you didn't want no trouble, Jed, and now you're——'

'Mrs Blair is a fine woman!' Niven cut in. 'She deserves to be courted by somebody better than a yellow high-born horse rancher who only gives a damn about what belongs to him!'

'You already said you hold the opinion I was wrong,' Steele said evenly, and not for the first time he was grateful for the decision to grow the beard because of how it made it easier to hide his true feelings sometimes. So long as he could keep his voice evenly pitched. 'Best you leave it at that, I reckon.'

'Yeah, Jed!' Bundy said tensely. 'If Steele don't get mad enough at you to do somethin' to shut you up, I figure I'll have to.'

'I'm through,' the embittered old man rasped between

clenched teeth. 'And I'm damn glad I've told him what I think of him to his face!'

'Okay with you if we leave now, mister?' Bundy asked, and hurled away the newly-lighted cigarette into the river. 'Now Jed's got all that off his chest?'

'Maybe you'd better do that,' Steele told him. 'Before I blow a hole in that chest he's just lightened.'

He slid his hand along the barrel of the Colt Hartford, fisted it around the frame, but continued to rest the stock on the seat so the muzzle was still aimed at the cloudless summer sky above the riverside glade in the timber.

Niven flicked the reins across the backs of the team and as the rig started forward he muttered loudly enough for his grim-toned voice to sound above the clop of hooves and turning of wheels: 'If you wanted to, you could shoot me in the guts, Steele! Least I got some!'

'Easy!' Bundy snarled.

The Virginian knew the shotgun rider was addressing his partner, but anyway rasped through gritted teeth, only loud enough for his own ears: 'Sure would be, but I reckon it'd be hard for me to live with.'

3

The southern boundary of the spread was something less than a half mile up the spur, where there was a five bar gate under a square arch in which the words TRAIL'S END were lettered in lengths of tree branch with the bark still on them.

When Steele reached this entrance to his place, climbed down off the wagon, opened the gate, drove through and paused again to re-close the gate, he was still mulling over in his mind the exchange with Jed Niven. And as he set the flatbed rolling again, he spat off the side then snarled in the tone of an expletive:

'People!'

It had been his aim when he first took the decision to look for a place to re-create something like the Steele Plantation in far off and long ago Virginia, to find a spot a lot of miles distant from the nearest town. Far enough off the beaten track so he would only ever come up against his fellow men if he chose. And maybe, he had even thought, he could succeed in making himself entirely self-sufficient: never have need to meet another living soul.

But he had always known that was nothing but a fantasy. That in this ever- and fast-changing world, a man could not exist entirely in isolation, forsaking his own kind, unless he became a total recluse: cut off by many secret miles from his nearest neighbour, living off game and wild crops.

Which kind of life would be far removed from anything he had experienced back in Virginia when the times had been so good. And he never had lost the taste for a rich lifestyle while he drifted from one frontier outpost to the next. Was often regarded contemptuously as a dude for the way he clung to a stylish mode of dress and indulged himself in living high off the hog when his bankroll allowed.

So the existence of a hermit, denying himself every pleasure in life except for life itself and the freedom to commune with nature unimpaired by the constraints of society, had never really been an option. It was as much a dream that could never come true as was the ambition to recreate his lost birthright.

But the compromise of Trail's End had a great deal to commend it. And he got along with most of the people he came into contact with in the Providence River Valley. Likewise the majority of passing through strangers.

The people like Ruth Blair, who he maybe would like to get to know better, far out-numbered the Jed Niven kind: who could sometimes corner him into reacting in the way he had as an over-indulged and quick-tempered rich kid before the war. Then the embittered, quick-to-kill man he had been trained to become as a Rebel cavalry lieutenant fighting the Yankees.

But mostly, his determination to build on the kind of life he had established for himself in the Providence River Valley enabled him to draw back from taking any violent step that would endanger all he had worked so hard to achieve.

Which was why he had not allowed the incident at the fork in the trails to rile him to such an extent that he got even close to goading Jed Niven into a kill or be killed stand-off: the odds of age and gunmanship heavily stacked in Steele's favour.

He drove the wagon off the end of the spur trail, emerged from thick-growing timber to start along the five hundred feet long track that ran between a field of wheat on the left, mixed vegetable crops on the right.

The house that bounded the yard on the east looked better than ever, now the bedroom he'd added on at the rear had weathered to match the much older timber and fieldstone of what had once been a single room shack. It looked particularly good since Al Strachen had painted the door and the window frames.

The combination barn and stable on the north side of the yard and the corral fence to the west had also been repainted by the hired hand.

Which was no big deal, Steele reflected as he drove across

the yard. He took more pride in the appearance of his place than most small farmers and ranchers in the valley and the businessmen in town. And he would have gotten around to sprucing up the buildings, done them as well as Strachen. But they would have had to take their places in line behind the more pressing work of caring for the breeding stock and raising the foals that earned him his daily bread and paid off the loan from Ethan Brady's bank.

As he reined the horse to a halt out front of the closed barn door he could count eight horses, mares and young, widely scattered over the area of pasture between the corral and Rocktop Hill. So there were a dozen more, including a stallion, roaming the lush grassland on the rolling hill country that comprised most of the spread: kept from straying off the place by the wire fencing strung out along every boundary line.

As he began to unload the sacks of feed supplied by Matthew Cody, he saw a few of his hens scratching around in the area beween the side of the house and the barn, not far from the low mound on the bank of the creek which marked the grave of Billy Baxter.

And he could hear the hog rooting in his pen out back of the barn, also the clucking of the other hens and the rooster someplace out by the pen.

He could neither hear nor see the milk cow, but she was free to graze anywhere on the spread, although she usually stayed in the area between the barn and the sinkhole that ensured Trail's End would never be short of water if Timber Creek ever dried up at a time of drought.

He did not expect to see Al Strachen. For the hired hand had asked for the day off to go on a private errand to Broadwater. Something he had done three times previously during the four weeks or so he had been working for Steele.

To do some drinking and some whoring and maybe some gambling in the places along Front Street, Steele suspected. But he had never asked the reason for the man's visits to the wide open town on the lake shore and Strachen had never volunteered any information. And since he never got paid for the hours he was away and always came back sober and ready for work again, Steele did not regard it as any of his business.

After he put the wagon in the barn and set the horse free to roam the pasture, he carried his grocery store and meat market purchases to the house. And as he entered the cool shade of its interior he was once again mildly troubled by the absence of a woman at Trail's End. Though right then he did not think in terms of the Widow Blair: a beauty with the kind of statuesque form that could make the prospect of a hermit's life seem more like a nightmare than a dream!

Not for the first time as he stepped into the empty house, he missed having Arlene Forrester around. The black woman who, like Lavinia Attwood the schoolteacher, and Billy Baxter the retarded man in his thirties with the mind of a child, had been among the few people to take to him when he first showed up in the Providence River Valley. And had lent a hand with the chores around the place when he started to get Trail's End into shape.

Like Billy, Arlene was dead now. And it caused Steele to experience a stab of shame that she had been dead for long enough so he only missed her at times like this. When there was no fire in the stove, no fragrance of fresh made coffee wafting out of the chimney with the scent of woodsmoke: nor any aroma of Arlene's fine cooked food filling the room.

But it was no great hardship to rustle up for himself a middle of the day meal from a few ingredients which had been in the store cupboard awhile, and some of the items freshly bought in town this morning.

He sat at the pine table in the kitchen part of the long room to eat the food and wash it down with coffee. And scanned the latest issue of the *Post-Despatch* which he had picked up from the grocery.

As usual, little of general interest had happened in the Providence River Valley over the past week: except for those readers who derived some sort of satisfaction from seeing familiar names in print because of some minor event that Attrill considered worthy of space in his columns. Which were less difficult to fill now the telegraph enabled him to collect and print statewide, national and even international news.

But last week it seemed there had been a lack of noteworthy incidents all around the world. So Steele never became deeply engrossed in anything within the pages of the newspaper. And was aware of slow-moving hooves and turning wheels as soon as the sounds came close enough to be within earshot this quiet afternoon, reaching into the house through the doorway he had left open.

The sound of wheelrims meant it was not Al Strachen returning from Broadwater earlier than usual, unless he had bought himself a wagon. Which seemed unlikely.

Steele was not expecting anyone else at Trail's End today. Certainly had no reason to presume an unexpected visit would bring trouble, so he took the time to fold the newspaper, put his plate, cutlery and coffee cup in a bowl of water and went to the threshold of the front doorway without a glance at the Colt Hartford that leaned against the wall beside the door.

Even though the rig was still at the start of the track between the crop fields, he immediately recognised the solid-roofed, red-painted, two-seater buggy that Harlan Grout had acquired second hand to rent out. Knew it had GROUT VEHICLE HIRE printed in black beneath the window on each side panel.

The driver was sitting well back on the upholstered seat in the deep shade of the afternoon sun cast by the roof and it was not possible to see at a distance who had the reins of the single horse in the shafts.

But when the buggy had rolled halfway down the track, he was able to discern it was a woman. A blonde woman, wearing a pale blue dress with a black band encircling her left upper arm.

He swallowed hard then. And felt moist patches under his armpits, at the small of his back and on his palms. Tried to tell himself it was the heat of the afternoon that had suddenly opened his pores. But knew he was lying to himself and angrily recalled what he had told the old-timer stage driver about how he could tell as much truth as any lawman.

So he admitted that maybe he had broken out in a sweat because the last time an unaccompanied beautiful woman had come to Trail's End uninvited it had started carnally, gone through pain and ended in tragedy.

But that was another discomforting and irritating thought.

Partly because it was a lie of the most stupid kind—the kind a man tries to tell himself. Mostly because although Isobel Denton and the events she had triggered were undeniably a part of his past, he was calling her to mind only as an excuse.

In an attempt to fool himself into not feeling foolish by admitting he had gotten hot and bothered because the driver of the buggy was the widow woman who had made such an instant impression on him when she emerged from the stage in Providence this morning.

'Mr Steele? Mr Adam Steele?'

He had stepped out of the doorway as she steered the buggy into a tight turn and now rolled it to a halt a few feet away. Leaned forward to look around the side panel; to see him and be seen by him in the flesh rather than through the dusty window.

When her expression altered from a bright smile to a look of curiosity he realised he was taking too long to respond to the straightforward query.

'That's me, Mrs Blair,' he answered after maybe a two-second delay, during which he had worried about how his voice might sound and what kind of unbidden expression had spread across his bearded face.

Now the smile returned to her features and he felt an easy expression spread across his own face when he heard his voice was unstrained.

'Good, I thought this had to be the place I was directed.'

She put on the brake, wound the reins around the lever and came down out of the buggy, a purse clutched in one hand. The purse was black, like the armband. A coincidence, or a substitute fashion accessory for the hat she no longer wore, he wondered. It was an irrelevant and maybe irreverent thought, but it served for a moment or two to keep his mind free of even more foolish and vastly more disrespectful notions concerning Ruth Blair.

'My, it's certainly a relief to reach the end of a long and tiring journey,' she went on, smiling more brightly as she brushed trail dust off the full skirts of her dress.

Close up, he saw her large eyes were blue, her lips were not so full as he had thought on first, distant impression and there were some grey strands among the mass of blonde in her long,

31

elegantly waved hair. She wore less paint and powder than before, so the lines at the side of her mouth and her eyes and at her throat showed up more clearly. But he thought she still looked a youthful forty: or, maybe, she was a year or two older.

Her hands were smooth and well cared for, which he chose to guess offered a clue to what the flesh of her body was like under her all-concealing garb. Her figure was less full than he recalled, but she still had plenty of feminine curves in all the right places.

While he made his appraisal of her, he was disconcertingly aware that she was also taking stock of him. But while he attempted to build up an impression with a series of unobtrusive glances, she peered long and hard at him.

'You came all the way from Denver to find me, Mrs Blair?' he asked.

She vented a short laugh, said: 'My name and where I'm from have travelled this far in such a short time? The way news is spread in country communities never ceases to amaze me. But no...'

She took a step closer to Steele, and reached into her purse. Took out a pair of spectacles and put them on. Laughed again, this time like she was embarrassed, before she offered an explanation for her apparent shamelessly open study of him earlier.

'You must please forgive me, Mr Steele.'

'Mrs Blair?'

She hurriedly removed the glasses, folded them and put them back in her purse. 'For not recognising you at once. I thought you looked familiar, but... You were in town this morning when the gallant Mr Fallows defended my good name?'

'A whole lot of men would have done the same thing if they were standing where the sheriff was, Mrs Blair.'

'Ruth. Call me Ruth, please?'

She gave another laugh which Steele hoped was not a kind she indulged in often. Because it made her sound and look like a foolish schoolgirl, which was not flattering to a woman of her age.

'You want to come inside out of the sun, Ruth?'

'That will be another welcome relief, Adam. If I may? Call you Adam, I mean.'

'In exchange for Ruth, sure,' he told her with a grin and thought he probably sounded like a schoolboy, notwithstanding the bushy beard.

When he stepped out of her path she moved inside the house and expanded on what she had started to explain.

'My eyesight is perfectly fine at distances. Better than most people's. But close to I need my eyeglasses. And I'm ashamed to admit vanity keeps me from wearing them most of the time in public, I'm afraid. And ... Oh, what a charming home you have, Adam.'

She halted a couple of paces over the threshold, and hurried to put on her glasses once more: looked carefully around to confirm her first blurred impression.

'It's a man's place,' Steele pointed out, annoyed with himself that it sounded like he was making an excuse for the familiar furnishings.

Which were comprised basically of the essential household chattels of a disenchanted couple who had left the frontier to go back east. Along with other items he had secured more recently at an auction sale in Broadwater. These later pieces of furniture, ornaments and pictures had belonged to a man who, like Steele, had lived alone.

The newly added bedroom was furnished in similar masculine style. It was reached through a doorway in the rear wall of the parlour, at present firmly closed.

'That is quite clear to see and is as it should be, Adam,' Ruth Blair said, unwittingly cutting in on the unbidden thought about the bedroom. She made another survey of her surroundings, nodded several times and murmured an occasional word of admiration. 'And done with surprisingly good taste, if you don't mind that I say so?'

She turned to look at him with undisguised approval, peering long and hard at him through the magnifying lenses of her spectacles: so she had no excuse of shortsightedness now.

'Go ahead,' he said with a small shrug.

'You are obviously a man who appreciates the finer things of life.'

'I like what I like.' It sounded trite and inadequate, then he seemed to plead poverty when he added: 'Whenever I can afford it.'

She nodded emphatically, then made a sound of irritation. 'Heavens, I must sound so patronising. But I have to say how much I admire how you maintain this standard of comfortable living. I'd only expect to find something like this back east. Or in San Francisco. Or in Denver, or...'

She broke off, shook her head, uttered a louder exclamation of self-disgust. Muttered with feeling: 'Yes, I am sounding patronising! Please forgive me again?'

Steele knew if she had had not struck a chord so deep within him at first impression, he would have taken angry offence at her attitude: because of her implication that because he was a Western horse rancher, he was expected to be a Philistine in terms of the finer things of life.

'You're not bothering me,' he assured her. Which was only a lie in terms of how it would not be polite for him to confide precisely just how she had been troubling him since he first recognised her as the driver of the buggy a few minutes ago.

'Oh, I'm sure I am,' she countered, still clearly annoyed at herself. She took off her spectacles and returned them to her purse.

'No, I——'

'I mean as a prattling woman so kindly invited into the domain of a bachelor, Adam. Let me tell you why I'm here and——'

'I just made coffee awhile ago, Ruth,' he cut in, over-anxiously. 'Won't take a minute to reheat the pot.'

'That would be most welcome, Adam. I had a fine lunch at the Knight boarding house. Shared with the local school-teacher... Miss Attwood, is that right?'

Steele had gone to the kitchen area of the room, to stir the embers in the stove into flames, as the woman sat in the chair beside the window with the bookcase underneath. The chair where he liked to take his end-of-the-day ease, sometimes with memories, other times with hopes, more often with a book.

'Lavinia Attwood,' he confirmed.

'Yes, Lavinia. A most refined lady. It was she who told me

34

Albert was working at a ranch called the Trail's End. Employed by Mr Adam Steele. As soon as I heard this, I'm afraid I rather bolted down Mrs Knight's fine pot roast and failed to take dessert or coffee in my eagerness to rent a buggy and drive out here. Following the directions Miss Attwood gave me. But do you know something, Adam?'

'I didn't know Al was short for Albert,' he replied, and wondered if he was able to conceal his disappointment that it was the hired hand and not him the fine looking woman had come all the way from Denver to see. Which was crazy, Godamnit!

'No, I mean... Now I'm here, in the company of such a fine southern gentleman, enjoying your hospitality in this charmingly furnished house, I'm no longer in such a hurry to see dear Albert again.'

'The reason you came from Denver to see Strachen isn't so important?' he asked, a little tensely, unsure whether he had detected cynicism in the tone she spoke the endearment.

'It certainly doesn't seem so now,' she answered. And now he was certain he heard a new tone in her voice as she watched him move from the kitchen end of the room into the parlour, bringing one of the four chairs from around the pine table. It was a tone that signalled strength of purpose.

'But I need to know what it is,' Steele told her, unwilling to make the assumption that sprang immediately to mind. Even though he decided it was not vanity that kept her from putting on her glasses now. Maybe she received only a blurred impression as she peered at him after he sat on the hard-seated, straight-backed chair some ten feet away from her. But she already knew what he looked like and she could continue to gaze fixedly at him without it seeming improper to reveal her deep interest in him. He hoped.

'It's a personal matter, Adam,' she said, not put out by what he asked, but maybe ready to be so if he pursued the issue.

'Al Strachen's worked here for a while, Ruth. We get along well. He's a good man to have around the place when there's chores to be done. If you're bringing him trouble, I don't want to give you any help to——'

She vented a deep, womanly laugh. Then shook her head,

35

said: 'Men! Oh, you men! I wish sometimes women would align themselves so loyally together. No, Adam, there's no trouble. Unless you count the untimely passing of Eversly Blair. Who Albert never liked from the start. Which was an opinion I grew to share over the years. So Albert won't consider my husband's death as anything but a cause for celebration.'

'Oh,' Steele said, which sounded as inadequate as he felt.

'I'm sorry for making light of a man's death, Adam. It embarrasses you, but I am not a hypocrite.'

'So you'll be joining Strachen in the celebration, Ruth?'

She peered even harder at him. Leaned closer to gaze with her weak eyes squeezed almost closed in concentration as he stood up when the coffee pot started to bubble. Thought she saw, and perhaps did see a frown of disappointment on Steele's bearded face.

'It will be a family celebration, Adam. Albert Strachen is my brother.'

'Your brother?' he repeated, and felt suddenly crazily happy.

She laughed, sharing his pleasure. 'Yes. I was born Ruth Strachen. I became Ruth Blair by making the most awful mistake of my life. Although, when I think about it sometimes, it can seem like most of my life has been one long mistake.'

'I'll get the coffee, Ruth,' he said as he turned away from her.

'If that's what you really want to do, Adam.'

'Uh?' He turned toward her again, and saw he had not misheard her tone of voice. The hint of self-pity that had started to sound as she spoke of the past had switched to innuendo, he thought. And now he saw the smile of invitation far removed from any kind of subtle hint.

She said, a throaty sound of sexual desire in her voice: 'I'm sure it would be perfectly correct if we had coffee, Adam. But I think we will both enjoy it more if first you make a mistake?'

4

It had been a long time since the last time for Adam Steele and in such a situation it would have been easy to think that with Ruth Blair it was the best time of all.

Maybe it was, and maybe it wasn't.

But it was sure different with her, and he was pretty damn sure it was one of the best times he had ever shared in a bed with a woman with such a fine body, a fine way with her and the experience she put to such good and careful use.

Because they were both mature adults who had gone down the roads of sexual pleasure and gratification a time or two before, there were no side issues of fumbling embarrassment to overcome once the offer had been made and accepted. And once the initial surprise of what was happening had passed, there were no surprises.

Which Steele considered no bad thing.

In the small bedroom they undressed quickly, not feeling the need to draw the drapes across the windows hung with net curtains. So the east-facing room was pleasantly lit with daylight which was missing the harsh sun in the afternoon.

They looked at each other's gradually denuded bodies with natural curiosity. Drawing stimulation from what they saw without any immediate need to fondle or caress the naked flesh.

No words of endearment or admiration were spoken.

For his part, Steele certainly admired Ruth's long, slender legs below a torso just slightly out of proportion across the hips in relation to the breasts that were inevitably a little pendulous at her age, but were not so large that they had lost all firmness.

She was a luxuriant natural blonde: the only body hair she allowed to adorn her in the shape of the triangle at the base of her stomach that was as flat when she was standing as when she went to lay on the narrow bed.

With any other woman, or perhaps if Ruth were not so myopic, Steele would have been perturbed by the way she peered so fixedly at him while he undressed: like she did not want to tear her gaze away from him for fear she missed something. And when he was naked, her gaze raked the length of his lean and lithe body several times, lips slightly apart as she breathed faster and heavier.

Her mounting excitement acted to heighten his own desire for her unblemished body, so he was ready to begin the act as soon as he placed himself between her splayed legs. Felt the twin pressures of her breasts against his sparsely-haired chest, then her hands on his back, gentle but somehow demanding as they roamed up and down his spine.

He lowered himself into her and she moved under him. He cupped his hands beneath her shoulder blades and she pressed harder with a clawed hand at the base of his spine, with the other steered his bearded face into the crook of her neck.

Their bodies were slick with a light sheen of sweat and soon the scent of her perfume was swamped by the musk of sexual desire.

'Yes,' she murmured softly, the first word she had spoken since he showed her into the bedroom. Said it after the thrust that drove him into her to the full extent: like she was expressing satisfied acceptance that this was good enough for her.

His lips were open on the soft, firm flesh where her neck joined her shoulder, but the pressure of her hand forcing his face against her prevented him from making any comprehensible sound.

The bed creaked. The hens clucked. The water of Timber Creek gurgled. And it was good and comfortable sex with a widow woman who, if she had held her husband in small regard in many ways, had obviously enjoyed this side of her marriage. Unless she had taken such pleasures with another man? Or many other men?

Steele did not give a damn. The thought neither repulsed him nor triggered greater stimulation as he neared the peak of pleasure: maintained enough self control to match his pace to that of the woman beneath him.

It ended as well as it began.

He emptied into her and felt her own drenching wetness then the tremor that went through her from head to toe. Felt weak, but without any sense of guilt or regret or shame or fear or any other dark emotion of the kind he had experienced with women taken on short acquaintance, maybe never to be taken again.

'That was wonderful, Adam,' she said as she let go of the back of his head and released the pressure of her hand on the base of his spine. But then embraced him gently in her arms with just enough demanding force to imply she was not yet ready for him to leave her. 'Not the best, because I always hope the next time will be the best.'

'When you find him, you'll give up looking?'

She could have been insulted and just for a stretched second of silence he expected to feel her body become rigid beneath him. Then it was past and she said:

'I expressed myself badly. There have been only three men in my intimate life. My first love, then Eversly Blair and now you. All of them have fulfilled my needs this way. I have never been disappointed. You must think I'm rather wanton, Adam? But I ask you to believe those three men are the only ones who have experienced me in such a brazen attitude.'

She let go of him and when he rose and stood beside the bed, she peered at him with her short-sighted eyes squeezed until they were almost closed again when he said:

'I believe you, Ruth. If that's important to you?' He stooped, started to pull on his pants.

'I'd like to think it's important to you, Adam.'

'That, too.'

She reached down to pick her dress up off the floor, draped it over her body like a bedcover.

'I'll go fix the coffee,' he said, scooped up the rest of his discarded clothing. 'It sounds and smells like it ought to be hot and strong by now.'

'Adam,' she called as he reached the doorway.

He paused on the threshold between the bedroom and the parlour, turned and saw the look on her face was as solemn as the tone of her voice. Like she was on the brink of telling him the greatest truth of all: revealing some earth-shattering fact that could alter the rest of their lives.

'Ruth?'

'The first time was with a boy who lived on the same street as us for twenty years. In Philadelphia. We used to go to the same church. He played on our swing in our yard when we were small children. Later we went to chaperoned socials dozens of times before I allowed him a first kiss.'

'I believe you, Ruth.'

She moved her head from side to side on the pillow, insisting she was not yet through. 'Eversly Blair did not put a hand on me intimately until the night of the day we married. Do you understand what that means, Adam?'

'It means a lot to me, Ruth.' Because he thought she expected so much more from him, it seemed like the most inadequate response he had offered her so far.

'It means you mean a whole lot to me, Adam,' she murmured.

'Ruth, I——'

She sat up in the bed, clasping the dress modestly in front of her body. 'No, you don't have to make any decisions. But if you want me to go, I'll leave right away. You can tell Albert I'm in town, waiting for him?'

'Ruth, I——' he tried again.

'Please, let me get it said,' she cut in. 'Before you start to think of me as a nag as well as a prattling woman. I'm almost done. I was about to add, or you can ride out to where Albert is working. And by the time the two of you get back to the house, I'll have fixed us a much more palatable pot of coffee than that stewing on the stove right now?'

Steele felt mildly shocked that Ruth Blair was unaware her brother had gone for the day: had believed he could have strolled in at any time on what was happening in the bedroom.

'Al's in Broadwater,' he told her. 'He doesn't usually get back until supper time.'

A bright smile broke across her face that had been solemn for so long. And she fixed the dress under her chin so it could not fall away after her hands were free to clap several times as she exclaimed: 'Oh, that's even better! You can do whatever work you have to do until supper time. By then I'll have fixed all of us—Albert, too—the finest meal I can rustle up out of what's in your store cupboards?'

Steele wished she would not clap her hands that way. And not squeal like that when she was excited. It was as irritatingly childish as her laughter could be sometimes.

Then he suddenly recalled the time the much younger Isobel Denton had cooked him a meal at Trail's End. But because he felt so content, fully satisfied by all that had happened since this more mature woman came here, his body refused to respond to a brief attempt to recall the degree of pain he suffered as a direct result of that night when the Denton girl came here.

But why the hell should it? Only he and the place were the same. The time and the circumstances and the woman were all different. Everything changes and a man should not always try to learn lessons for the future by paying too much attention to the past. If he had done that, he would never have taken the decision to settle here at Trail's End.

'Well?' she asked.

He looked at her, saw her nervously expectant look change to a smile that matched the expression which came to his own face as he decided the ability to cook well could cancel out her irritating habit of sometimes acting like an overgrown schoolgirl.

'Sounds good, Ruth.'

'Then skedaddle, mister,' she urged, laughed like a woman and made a dismissive gesture of her head now she was again holding the dress up in front of her with her hands. 'There are times when a lady enjoys being watched when she undresses. But I don't think anybody gains anything from watching her get dressed again.'

'Suppertime at Trail's End is generally around seven,' he told her.

'Then that gives us both plenty of time to do what we have to do. I'll expect you back in time to wash up and be at the table at seven?'

'Count on it. If Al gets back from Broadwater with time to spare, you can tell him I'll be working on the fence up beyond High Point Hill. That's if you don't spend all the spare time talking over family business?'

He went through into the other room to finish dressing.

She called out to him: 'When I'm in the kitchen, Adam, I consider myself an artist. And an artist does not like to be distracted by the mundane when she is working on her current masterpiece.'

Steele could not sing well, and he seldom attempted to carry a melody during the many more hours he was alone than when he was in the company of others. But he hummed and la-laed and sometimes broke out into a breathy whistling of some indefinable tune as he took the horse and buggy hired from Harlan Grout across to the barn, freed the horse from the shafts and led him into a stall, ensured there was feed and water for the animal. Then he put his own gelding back in the traces of the flatbed, loaded two reels of barbed wire on the wagon and drove outside into the sunlight.

When he glanced at the house, he could not decide if there was more or less smoke rising from the chimney. But he saw a fleeting movement of something bright behind the window at the parlour side of the central doorway. Which was perhaps a glimpse of Ruth's dress as she crossed the room. Though he hoped, as he drove off the yard through the gap between the corner of the corral and the side of the barn, it was the flick of a dusting cloth.

He could, without too much distaste, cope with most of the chores normally undertaken by women in a house: except using a duster. He did not feel right doing it, and he always rushed it: inevitably did not clean the house as thoroughly as he would have liked.

Then he endeavoured to banish from his mind thoughts about Ruth Blair and what she was doing in his house as he drove without haste across the pasture where there were now a dozen of his twenty bloodstock horses grazing.

They looked as contented with their lot as Steele felt with his. Were obviously enjoying the good grazing in the freedom of the open air that was not so hot this afternoon as this morning. There was even a bank of grey cloud shrouding the distant ridges of the Sierra Nevadas to the east, which maybe signalled summer rain later in the afternoon or in the evening. Which would do no harm to the rolling acres of Trail's End.

That was one aspect of the Providence River Valley he liked

better than his childhood home back in Virginia. When it rained in summer here, it was a good, cooling, refreshing rain that brought relief to every living creature. With none of the sticky, mouldy-smelling humidity that in Virginia can be more tiring than a day of blistering sun.

He counted five more free-roaming horses as he drove to the far north west corner of the property, rolling near the end of the ride through three feet high grass that soon would need to be cut for winter fodder.

But he was not concerned that three horses were missing from his cursory count: knew they were surely hidden from sight in a fold of the hills or one of the stands of timber which featured the spread between Rocktop Hill with the granite slab balanced on its crest and High Point Hill, topped by a thicket of trees.

Because he had been supplied by mail order with substandard material, the barbed wire strung out a hundred feet to the south and two hundred feet to the east at the corner behind High Point had rusted badly in a short time. Al Strachen should have been replacing the bad wire today, but he had gone to Broadwater instead and the work had been rescheduled for tomorrow.

But the chores Steele had in mind to undertake this afternoon when he returned from Providence were concentrated close to the house. And he had decided it would be better to keep away from there, take account of Ruth's remark about not wanting to be distracted: for although he did not consider himself an artist at anything he did, he would sure have been affected in what he was doing if he could see or hear her so soon after they...

He again made a conscious effort to keep thoughts of the woman out of his mind. And succeeded in doing so throughout the bright, warm afternoon while he prised the old staples out of fence posts, removed the rusted strands of wire and replaced them with new lengths.

Once, one of his roan Arabian mares which had always been the most affectionate animal in his string, came cantering up and stayed cropping the grass nearby for awhile before she drifted off again. The gelding from out of the wagon traces whinnied his wish to go with her, but was held by the hobbles.

Steele did not own a pocket watch, largely because there were few occasions in his daily life when it was necessary to have anything but a rough idea of what time it was. Often, hunger was a good enough yardstick to judge the passing of the hours .And on a fine summer day like this, the advance of the sun across the sky, still cloudless in the west although it was gradually filling with grey from the east, was a more accurate guide.

When he completed his work on the fences, he judged he had more than an hour to spare until Ruth Blair's deadline. Which included the time it would take him to get to the house near the opposite corner of the property, wash up—maybe even trim his beard this evening, he thought—and change into a clean shirt before he sat down at her table.

No, damnit, he corrected himself with a twinge of irritation. At his table, to eat his food that happened to have been cooked by her. He was too damn eager to give Ruth Blair a bigger part in his life than she was entitled to on such short, albeit intimate, acquaintance.

It was easy enough to fill this spare time pleasantly while he allowed the woman to direct his life to the extent of abiding by the time scale she had laid out.

He trudged up to the top of High Point Hill from where it was possible to command a panoramic sweep of more of Trail's End than anywhere else on the spread.

But the house and its immediate surroundings were hidden from sight from here, because of the form the land took in that direction. He knew from experience, though, that the smoke stain which smudged the sky in the distance was from the house chimney. And it was easy, as he sat on his haunches in the early evening shade of the timber, to imagine the kind of cooking smells that would be mingling with the aroma of woodsmoke.

This as he allowed his gaze to wander back and forth over the best part of the three thousand acres of his horse ranch in his sight. At one time counted all twenty of his bloodstock horses scattered far and wide.

But otherwise he kept his mind a blank, a sense of contentment suffusing him as he relished his achievement in making Trail's End such a good place, stocked with the very best animals he had been able to buy, after hard horse trading, without getting too deeply into debt at Ethan Brady's First Providence Town Bank.

He was still content when at length he rose from where he had been hunkered on his haunches, and started down the hill. Just as the slow-moving belt of cloud finally overhauled the sinking sun, watered it to pale yellow so it was no longer dangerous to look at. Content, but not complacent.

For that was a lesson, repeated time and again throughout his past life as a drifter, that he had finally learned to apply to the future. Knew that when all looked to be fine and dandy and you had a rock steady, secure hold on everything you worked for, that's when Lady Luck is most likely to quit smiling on you all of a sudden, lose all her airs and graces, and kick you smack in the teeth.

After he set off to drive back to the house, the sky grey and the evening air cooling, he reflected that he had also learned to keep concern about this risk in proportion. For most of the time, his awareness of what the cruel fates could do to him was stowed deep at the back of his mind. To have it otherwise, be constantly nagged by doubt about the future and what lay in wait there... That was self-defeating and he had endured more than enough of being his own worst enemy.

The first spots of light rain splattered as he drove within sight of the house. And not for the first time he glanced at the clouds in the darkening sky, decided they were too high and thin to threaten a thunder and lightning storm that could panic highly bred horseflesh, drive the animals into headlong bolts that could damage them.

He knew this was a rational decision: that unless the weather took a turn for the worse, there was no need to round up his stock, drive them into the corral or even the stable section of the barn, to protect them from the ill effects of their own potential panic.

He had to think this way: in terms of being reasonable and getting his priorities right. For he could see the corral, the barn at one side, the crop fields at the other and the house behind the yard. Imagined he could smell the woodsmoke, even hear meat sizzling in a skillet on the stove. He could certainly see lamplight gleaming at the two front windows, these squares of yellow illumination completing the warmly welcoming aspect of home. Especially to a man already uncomfortably wet and likely to be soaked through to the skin by the time he got to the end of the drive.

But he was not entirely entranced by this spell. He was no fool. If he truly considered his stock was in the slightest danger, the house and all the good things it contained would have had to wait.

God, he felt good as he drove into the yard, the rain not heavy enough to yet soften the hard-packed surface, and he was able to devote more time to looking at the net-curtained, undraped windows than concentrating on driving the wagon. For the gelding was as anxious as he to get inside out of the wet: took the most direct line toward the closed doorway of the barn without need of any commands through the reins.

But he failed to see any sign of movement in the house. Which was maybe to be expected.

For Ruth would still be putting the finishing touches to supper in the kitchen end of the room, out of direct line of the window.

And Al Strachen, if he was back from Broadwater, could be with her. Or, more likely, he was taking his ease in the comfortably padded armchair in the other area of the room, slumped down so his head was below the level of the window sill.

But if either of them heard the sounds of the wagon and horse crossing the yard, rolling toward the barn, they did not come to a window. But it was raining harder now and the beat of the drops on the roof of the house surely covered the less than obtrusive sounds as the flatbed came to a halt behind the buggy vividly labelled as belonging to Harlan Grout.

Steele indulged in some more unmelodious whistling as he climbed down off the wagon, took the gelding out of the traces, hauled open one of the double barn doors and started to lead the animal inside.

'Now!'

It was a man's voice. Low and tense and a little throaty, like he had intended for the single word to be snarled out with greater force.

Steele became silent and froze as a match was struck in compliance with the order. He was blinded for a moment to

46

everything except the brilliant flare in the darkness. Off to the right, in the stable area of the building. Then the flame softened and a moment later that part of the barn was filled with light when the wick of a kerosene lamp ignited, the chimney was dropped in place.

'I'll kill you if I have to, Steele!' Strachen warned, the initial catch gone from his throat now. His voice and his attitude were coolly commanding as he levelled a Colt .45 at Steele from twenty feet away to the left. To emphasise the validity of his threat, he thumbed back the hammer of the revolver, thrust it forward with his elbow slightly bent, aimed at the Virginian's chest.

'He means it, Adam!' Ruth Blair gasped from where she stood beside the lamp she had lit, hung from a rope tied to a rafter.

She looked as miserably ashamed of what she was doing as her brother looked grimly capable of carrying out the threat on the slightest provocation.

Steele let go the bridle of the gelding and raised his hands until they were level with his shoulders, a few inches to either side, said: 'I know it, Ruth.'

'I didn't——' she started to explain, on the verge of spilling tears down the tracks left by earlier weeping.

'You don't have to make excuses for a winning combination,' Steele cut in on her.

'It wasn't meant to be this way!' Strachen snarled. 'I never knew Ruth was going to show up around here!'

'But you should stick with it, feller.'

'I didn't——' Ruth tried again.

'In the books of a lot of people, it's the secret of success, feller.'

'You're not making any sense, Steele.'

'Sex and violence, Strachen.' Steele switched his unblinking gaze between the brother and sister as he went on: 'You're threatening me with violence and this makes twice in one day she's screwed me.'

5

Al Strachen directed a glowering glance at his sister and demanded to know: 'What's this man talking about, Ruth?'

Then he shook his head vigorously and returned his blazing-eyed gaze to where Steele stood in the barn doorway, dripping wet, impassive, not moving a muscle. He was angry at himself because of the way he had dropped his guard as he questioned his sister. Got angrier still when he realised he did not need to hear Ruth confirm something he could work out for himself.

Steele was relieved he had not tried to take advantage of Strachen's mistake. For as the gazes of the two men locked, it was obvious that one needed just the slightest excuse to gun down the other: and the other knew it.

'Never mind!' Strachen growled after a two second pause during which the tension built up an almost palpable presence in the barn that was filling with cool, damp-smelling night air streaming in through the open doorway where the Virginian and the gelding stood. 'I'm a United States marshal, Steele. Putting you under arrest for murder.'

Steele was abruptly certain the immediate threat of his violent death had passed. Which freed his mind to trigger a sinking feeling that he knew to just which murder his erstwhile hired hand referred as he responded: 'I can see what you are, feller.'

Strachen was in his late twenties, maybe already thirty. He had a six-feet-tall, rangy build that Steele had never seen move at anything faster than a carefully even pace. But in back of everything the man did, there was always a suggestion he could swing into faster action if the situation demanded it. This was never more apparent than now.

His face, which showed no family resemblance to that of

48

Ruth, was good-looking in a well worn, lived-in way. In repose it wore a hangdog look of the kind Steele had always supposed some women found appealing: anyway, those kind of women who liked to mother their men, no matter what the age or the woman or the man.

And as he looked at the grim-set features now, with the bags under the brown eyes, down-turned lines at the sides of the thin, slightly-twisted mouth, the nose that was just a degree off centre, Steele wondered if this kind of attraction to women was the Strachen male line's equivalent of the childish traits Ruth occasionally exhibited.

This evening, Strachen was attired as he always had been when he took a trip to Broadwater. In a three-piece, dark-hued suit that fitted him too tightly, as did his Derby hat which was a size too small because it did not take account of his dishevelled brown hair that was in need of cutting when he first showed up at Trail's End looking for work.

He had taken the precaution of being ready to back the announcement he planned to make as soon as Steele entered the barn and he sprang his trap: wore a United States marshal's badge pinned to the left hand side of his vest front, the suit jacket open to display the silver coloured six pointed star within a circle.

'And don't make any mistakes about me, Steele,' he growled. 'I've been in this line of business too long to let myself be unsettled by anything a prisoner can say to me.'

Steele knew there was nothing even faintly funny about the situation, so this was not some elaborate joke. And since he had been fully awake since dawn and had total recall of everything that had happened during the day, he did not for a split second consider this could be some kind of bad dream.

But there remained a sense of unreality within the barn as he continued to come to terms with the effects of being so badly jolted by the totally unexpected revelation: that the good-natured, easy-going, less-than-bright Al Strachen was a lawman, come to arrest him.

More than the prominently displayed badge and the menacing hardness of his demeanour, the strongest evidence of the complete turn-around of the man was the way Strachen spoke Steele's name without the deferential *mister* prefix he

49

had always insisted on previously.

Steele said: 'I reckon a lot of them ask you if you've got a warrant, Al... Marshal?'

'Yes! Yes, he has, Adam. Albert is——'

'Ruth!' Strachen snapped, harsh with ill temper as his expression suddenly became closer to the human equivalent of an enraged timberwolf than any other kind of dog in any other mood.

This time he let his gaze shift from Steele to Ruth for just a part of a second. Then he looked back at the Virginian with the same expression still in place. Took as long as two seconds to bring his anger under control so his voice was no longer a snarl when he said: 'Ruth, please. Just do like I tell you, honey. First off, what you promised you would do?'

The woman vented a small, strangled sound: like a groan of pain, or maybe a moan of anguish.

Steele looked at her, conscious of her brother's gaze fixed upon him like it was tangible, reaching out to press into his face. And he saw Ruth's expression was a match for the degree of depthless misery that had sounded in her throat.

She advanced on him, and brought into sight the hand that she had been careful to hide behind her back ever since she showed in the lamplight. Over the partially folded palm there was draped a three feet long length of the same rope which had been used to suspend the lamp from the rafter.

Strachen instructed grimly: 'Want you to turn your back on her, put your hands behind you so she can tie them, Steele. And you keep in mind what I told you, Ruth. Don't put yourself between him and me. And Steele, you make any move for the knife in your boot, I'll kill you. The warrant states dead or alive. I prefer to bring in my prisoners alive.'

'Please, Adam, don't make him kill you!' Ruth pleaded.

Steele drawled sardonically: 'In this matter, lady, me and your brother have the same preference.'

'God, this is awful,' she murmured as Steele turned his back on her and lowered his hands, placed them behind him with the wrists together, making it easy for her to do as her brother had instructed.

Steele said in the same ironic tone as before: 'Seems I share another opinion with another member of the Strachen family.'

'Good and tight now, Ruth,' Strachen urged as the woman looped the rope around Steele's wrists. 'Like I told you. Remember, he's nothing like he seems to be. He's a cold-blooded killer and you don't have to feel——'

'I said I'd do it!' she snapped shrilly at him.

'And I believed you,' he countered, a little tensely. 'But that was before I knew you and he had——'

'For heaven's sake, I couldn't help myself!' Ruth shrieked, anguish close to tears in her shriller, more tremulous voice.

Then she vented a cry, similar to but more forceful than earlier. Snatched the rope away from Steele's wrists. Sidestepped to place herself between the levelled gun and Steele. Then shoved him sideways with both hands, screamed: 'Run, Adam! Get away from him! I can't help him to do this to you!'

Steele could do nothing but respond to the power of her thrusting hands, almost pitched to the ground at the threshold of the barn as he was unbalanced. His mind raced as he struggled to stay on his feet.

He had always been aware this was not a cruel joke nor a bad dream. Knew with equal certainty that nothing which had been said or done in the barn since the order to light the lamp was given was triggered by anything less than genuine emotion.

Marshal Albert Strachen fully intended to arrest him for murder. Or kill him if he resisted.

Ruth Blair had been caught in a dilemma because of her feeling for Steele and that for her brother. And whether she held any opinion concerning the morality of Steele's crime and the lawman's duty to see justice was done was immaterial. She had now come down on the side of the wrongdoer: aligned herself against her own brother.

And because Steele had seen the end of his new life—maybe the end of his mortal life—staring him in the face ever since Strachen announced his attention, there could be no doubt about what he should do with the opportunity provided him by the woman.

51

He stayed on his feet and took control of his own movement as the impetus of Ruth's shove was lost. Then bounced off the flank of the gelding, came out of the dry stable into the teeming rain.

The horse snorted a protest that almost drowned the sound of the lawman's voice, but not quite.

'—— crazy, lovesick, stupid woman!' Strachen roared. 'I could've killed you!'

His sister hurled at him: 'Maybe I'll end up wishing you had!'

Then the only sounds Steele heard were of the rain as it beat upon the buildings and the wagons, lashed at the ground, and the splashing of his own feet as he raced across the yard.

He felt almost uncontrollably enraged by what had happened. Especially because of how good his life had been before it was abruptly shattered. And he was more afraid than he could ever remember being in his entire life, despite the countless dangers of every kind he had faced previously.

Not so much afraid of going down in the mud with a fatal bullet in his back. Instead, of surviving without everything that had come to make life worth living for him.

But he forced himself to get a grip on the anger and the fear quickly: concentrated them into a tight ball that gave him a feeling of ice in the pit of his stomach. It was a well practised process he had not needed to utilise in a long time, that acted to clear his mind and had a sharpening effect on his reactions.

Immediately he realised it would be futile to make for the house. For the man who had pretended to be so slow-moving and slow-thinking when he acted the part of a hired hand was obviously not so in his true vocation of a United States Government appointed peace officer.

Strachen would not be sluggish in opening fire on his target illuminated by the lamplight in the house. And doubtless he would have confiscated and hidden the Colt Hartford he knew was always stowed against the wall beside the doorway when it was not within easy reach of its owner.

Steele ran between the front of the barn and the side of the house. Slithered into a turn to the left just short of the mound of Billy Baxter's grave. Moved between the side of the barn and Timber Creek, already higher and running faster as a result of the evening downpour.

He slowed to a walk, lowering the sound of his feet on the soggy ground. Heard Ruth's high-pitched voice forced into silence by the harshly-spoken words of her brother. Nothing either of them said reached Steele in a form he could comprehend.

Then the gelding snorted again. And for a few moments hooves thudded on the muddy surface of the yard when the animal was put to flight by something Strachen did to drive the horse out of the barn doorway. One of the doors slammed against the outside wall of the building, and Strachen's voice yelled loud and clear against the hiss of pouring rain:

'Steele! If you can hear me, you'd better listen good to what I'm saying! It's the James Bishop killing I'm arresting you for! And I'm not the only officer of the law knows you live here! You can maybe kill me, Steele, but there'll be others here in a couple of days! That's why I went to Broad——'

The Virginian moved around to the rear of the barn. Saw the motionless black and white shape of the Friesian milk cow. Smelled the hogpen. Heard the chickens clucking contentedly in the shelter of their coop.

Strachen's voice was still discernible, but the sense of what he was saying did not reach through the solid bulk of the barn and the sounds of the rain to register in Steele's mind. A mind that for stretched seconds teetered on the brink of panic as he struggled to overcome the compelling conviction that now he was in a dark, drenching, terror-filled dreamworld. From which he could gain release by giving vent to a piercing scream of helplessness.

But he struggled against losing his sense of reason. Knew he sometimes spoke aloud, but took care to restrain his voice to a whisper, as he told himself over and over that he was caught up in real events. It was like a waking nightmare sure enough: but one he had always known could become a reality. From that awful day when he rode away from the lifeless body of his best friend.

He shook his head violently and softly but vehemently muttered a string of obscenities into his beard. Cursed himself for allowing panic to get even a fingertip hold on him.

The time for panic was when he had been Strachen's

prisoner. In the custody of a United States marshal. Who would take him back east, to stand trial for Jim Bishop's murder. In Tennessee where Bish died. Or Virginia where they both hailed from. To maybe get acquitted: which was a hundred to one against chance! Much more likely to be found guilty. And sentenced to hang. Or serve a long prison term. Be set free in the distant future to return here...

Find Trail's End had degenerated into the ruin it had been when he found it...

Or been appropriated by somebody else, just as he had appropriated it...

Which could happen. He had no legal title to the land. And Ephraim Sanderson, who first settled here and gave it the name Trail's End had died before he could tell anyone other than Steele that he approved the Virginian having the place.

But that was a futile line of thinking, damnit! Because he was not going to be recaptured by Marshal Albert Strachen, have his fate put in the hands of a bunch of strangers who would have every legal and moral right to find him guilty.

But what was the alternative?

To run again! Just as he had been a fugitive after he killed Bish, started out on all those wasted years of drifting until he found the stability he had searched for here at Trail's End.

Halfway along the rear of the barn he halted and pressed his back against the wall. His back ached, his head felt on fire and ready to burst with the heat and he tasted acid bile that warned him he was going to get sick to his stomach if he did not retain a grip on himself. But in such a state of bone deep weariness that left him so dispirited, he was not sure he could do it.

When he started to circle the barn, it had been with a pre-conceived plan in mind.

In addition to the Colt Hartford, there was just one other firearm kept at Trail's End. An elderly and uncared for Frontier Colt which was stowed on a dusty shelf in the barn. In the old days this revolver had a specific purpose: on the infrequent occasions Steele was required at the house while he was working on a distant part of the spread, Billy Baxter or Arlene Forrester had instructions to discharge one shot into the air.

Since Strachen packed a holstered revolver of his own, it had not been necessary to tell him about the old Colt. Maybe he had noticed it there on the shelf during his time on the place, but even if that were so, he would likely have forgotten about it in his hurry to make Steele his prisoner. Capture him with a makeshift plan, probably. Put into hurried action when he unexpectedly found his sister so comfortably settled at Trail's End?

But now Steele found himself suddenly disinclined to make a try for the revolver. For if Strachen saw it in his hand, the lawman was likely to be pushed into a kill-or-be-killed showdown.

And just as Steele did not intend to give himself up, neither was he in any mood to hold his fire and thereby commit suicide. Nor, with a bunch of other US marshals on their way here, did he relish gunning down a government-appointed lawman. For he was already in plenty of trouble on a similar score—Bish had been a deputy sheriff back in Virginia all those years ago.

So, better to bide his time. Go to ground and wait for a less dangerous opportunity to reclaim the Colt Hartford. For that was the sole purpose behind the plan to obtain the old revolver and get the drop on Strachen. For if he was going to be dispossessed of everything else he owned by starting out a new life as a drifting fugitive, he was not going to do so without the rifle.

'Adam!'

The voice seemed to come from a long way off. Maybe from deep in the back of his mind, he thought.

'Adam, can you hear me?'

From out of the real world. Ruth Blair's voice, holding a quality of strangled shrillness, like she was trying desperately to shout as loud as she could, but was hampered by a physical or emotional tightness that constricted her throat.

He had been about to angle away from the rear of the barn: to go between the hogpen and the chicken coop, then cut to the side, splash through the creek that was still summer narrow and shallow despite the rain, easy to wade. Thence into the dense timber through which the barbed wire boundary fence was strung.

His planning had gone little further than this. Bogged down by futile memories of how he had helped the ill-fated Davy Clavell escape the lynch mob of vigilantes by a similar cross-country route. While, in the back of his troubled mind, there was an idea concerned with Crumpled Crag: the high point on the eastern side of the Providence River Valley where the doomed Cowper Loomis had attempted to hide out in a cave among the rocks.

'Adam, please hear me! Please listen!'

He was held in a frozen attitude, a half pace away from the wall of the barn. Her voice was clearer in the rain now. It was still strained, but he heard her shrill-toned words distinctly enough to detect a note of sincerity in them.

But was it a phoney emotion? Or did it simply sound fake because of the tension she was feeling?

'Albert can't harm you now! I want to help you, Adam! But you must trust me! Please come to me, Adam! Please!'

He had her pinpointed on the yard, and the next moment he turned to again follow the route he had intended when he started to circle the barn.

In the silence that followed her promise and entreaties, vividly remembered phrases came and went swiftly through his mind.

In the barn. *For heaven's sake, I couldn't help myself*, she had said. *I said I'd do it.* Her brother had trusted her, but she had not done it. *Crazy, lovesick woman*, Strachen had accused.

Earlier, in the bedroom, she had claimed so much she said was the truth. And he had promised to believe her. Especially: *It means you mean a lot to me.*

God, that wonderful, beautiful, incredible time in the house seemed a million years and a million miles away from this rain-sodden night as he stepped round the rear corner of the barn, moved cautiously along the side to the front corner. There pressed his back tight to the wall, craned his neck and leaned forward. Achingly tensed to draw back if he glimpsed a gun swing toward him.

Or, if the risk was worth taking, to scuttle into the inadequate but only available cover of the flatbed wagon and Harlan Grout's buggy parked on this side of the yard. Thence into the barn doorway. There to go straight to where the old Colt ought to be if Strachen had not put it with the Colt Hartford.

For Steele's mind had been changed again. Because if he could not trust Ruth Blair, then he wouldn't be able to trust anyone else as he spent the rest of his life hiding from the law. He'd have to be prepared to kill anyone who was a threat to his freedom. So he might as well start with Al Strachen. And his double-crossing sister, if that was what she turned out to be.

He inched his head far enough to the side to see her.

She had opened the house door so a third shaft of light supplemented those that shone from the flanking windows. Brightly illuminated her as she stood in the centre of the yard, arms hanging limply at her sides, dishevelled hair plastered to her face, the fabric of her dress adhering to the curves of her body.

Her brother was slumped at her feet and the teeming rain had not quite yet obliterated the track she had left on the muddy surface when she dragged him from the doorway of the barn to where he now lay.

Inertly in death? *Albert can't harm you now!* she had yelled. Or just unconscious? The curtain of fast-falling rain and the way the lamplight shimmered in the drops made such subtle details as the rise and fall of a man's chest impossible to discern at a distance.

It was also not possible to see if there were tears mixed with the raindrops running down Ruth's cheeks. But certainly her expression was of depthless misery.

He stepped out into the open, called to her: 'Ruth.'

She had started to tilt her head back, turn her face to the deluge from the sky: to plead again for Steele to come to her, or to pray for guidance. Now she snapped her head around to peer at the Virginian. Probably could not see him at first because he was beyond the fringe of light from the house.

She seemed startled close to terror. And he was suddenly in the grip of something similar as he realised the extent of the trust he had placed in this woman. Who had broken a promise to her brother, fully aware of the potentially fatal consequences to him. Maybe now she was making good the

57

lapse in family loyalty: acting a siren's supporting role while he played possum, waiting the right moment to spring into action, aim and fire a killing shot at Steele.

'Oh, thank God!' she gasped. She lifted one hand, gestured down at Strachen. 'I hit him, Adam! On the head! With a spade handle, oh God!'

Steele quickened his pace out of the darkness and into the lamplight. Came close enough to see that she had done flesh-splitting, blood-spilling damage to her brother's hatless head. But his chest was moving steadily up and down.

He said with a strained tone of manufactured irony, making what he knew was going to be a doomed attempt to ease the tension of the situation: 'Are you absolutely sure you come from Philadelphia, Ruth?'

She heard his voice, but clearly did not comprehend the words as she emerged from stunned shock, blurted: 'What?'

Steele was recovered enough from his own near terror to realise it would be cruel to make a joke at the woman's expense. He shook his head and moved his hand in a dismissive gesture, pitched his voice too low for her to hear him when he growled: 'Don't they call that the city of brotherly love?'

6

Steele did not waste any more time with bad jokes, and just a little on inaction when he came close enough to Ruth on the Trail's End yard to recognise in the rain-sparkling lamplight that she was on the brink of hysteria.

For perhaps a full ten seconds he held her in the downpour, his arms wrapped around her after she almost leapt away from her unconscious brother: rushed at him with a sound that was a mixture of a cry of near joyful relief and a wail of helpless anguish. Buried her tearful face into his shoulder as her body trembled, like she had a fever, and a string of sobs bubbled from her lips.

But even while he stood with her this way, one of his hands on the back of her head, moving gently in her sodden hair as he made what he hoped were comforting sounds in her ear, his mind considered and rejected several plans of action.

And he had decided on the only course open to him and was just a moment removed from taking the first step to implement it when Ruth regained control of herself. She pulled away from him and took hold of his hands in her own, pleaded:

'Tell me what we're going to do, Adam? I'll do anything you ask of me, I promise. Anything.'

She looked drained and sick. Older than her years. A world away from the woman he had seen step off the stage, climb out of the buggy, spread herself for him on his bed. But everything he ever thought of her on those occasions he felt manyfold more right then. And he knew she felt the same about him.

Then, after he told her what he intended, she started to prove she had not spoken empty words. And showed that she fully recognised the gravity of his situation: possessed an inner strength of purpose she could harness to transcend physical and mental suffering for as long as it took to help him.

With Steele, she carried her brother into the house and attended to the gash on his head. Then, while Steele was out of the house, she towelled Strachen dry and put him into bed.

While they were together she asked no questions. Neither did Steele. And except by an occasional grimace of remorse or frown of sympathy now the heat of the violent moment had gone, she made no comment on the snap decision to side with Steele against her brother to the extent of injuring him.

Steele had no time to spare for indulging in how he felt about being forced to turn his back on everything he had worked toward for so many years. Even when he was alone while Ruth watched over her brother with his own gun in case he woke up, he had no inclination to wallow in self pity. He sure enough felt the temptation, but he did not submit to it.

He led the gelding back from the far side of the yard where he had bolted, and for the third time that day put the animal in the traces of the flatbed. Threw the tangled bundles of rusted wire off the wagon.

When the rig was ready to roll, he returned to the house. Strachen was still unconscious, but his sister had used his pants belt to lash his wrists together at the front, his arms resting above the counterpane. His revolver was on the nightstand.

'If he did wake up, Albert would know I couldn't possibly shoot him, Adam,' Ruth explained. 'What I did to him before, that was just . . .' She shrugged.

Steele asked her if she knew what her brother had done with the Colt Hartford and she showed him where it was lodged behind the bookcase in the parlour.

'I'm grateful,' he told her, a little huskily. Rested the rifle on the arms of the easy chair while he got the rain slicker that hung on a peg behind the front door, put it on. 'You'll be all right?'

'Oh?' She looked and sounded crestfallen.

'Something wrong, Ruth?' He tried to tell himself he was a stupid fool for daring to hope he knew what it was.

'You're leaving me here?'

'You think your brother's likely to be mad enough at you to hurt you when he——'

She shook her head, directed a glance through the open doorway into the bedroom. 'No! No, Albert will be angry at me, but he'd never harm me. But I was hoping I could come with you, Adam.'

It was as if, at that moment, the greatest burden of his troubles was lifted. And he felt good enough in these seemingly worst of all possible circumstances to show a bright smile when he admitted: 'That's real strange, Ruth. I was hoping you'd want to come with me, too.'

The most fleeting of unstable smiles flitted across her face as they moved toward each other and she whispered:

'I told you, I'll do anything you want me to.'

They were ready to embrace again. Maybe to kiss this time. But Strachen gave a low groan, the first sound he had made except for his regular breathing since they brought him into the house.

'We'd better get moving, Ruth,' Steele urged. 'Another crack on the head so soon could do him serious damage. But I don't want to leave him tied up, in case ...'

'Let's go!' she broke in, a little harshly, and moved resolutely to the door, jerked it open and stepped out into the rain without looking back.

Steele went into the bedroom, where Strachen was twitching a little, groaning some more. But his eyelids stayed firmly closed and after a few moments he settled back into an unfeeling level of unconsciousness. He did not move nor make a sound as Steele removed the belt from around his wrists.

Then the Virginian gathered up the rest of Strachen's clothing, blew out the lamp and left the room, closing the door on the man who sounded like he was soundly asleep.

The fire in the stove had died down before the food could cook dry in the pots or the coffee boil over. This was the only detail Steele took conscious note of about the familiar room before he doused both lamps.

And he tried to tell himself it was not so much a lump in his throat as the dryness of the start of a cold or something that caused him the need to swallow hard as he stepped over the threshold and closed the door firmly behind him.

Ruth was already up on the passenger side of the wagon seat, hugging herself as the rain continued to fall steadily through the night air that was much colder than earlier.

'Is Albert all right?' she asked tautly.

'I reckon he's a lot more comfortable than you are right now, Ruth.'

'I'll be fine, once we're moving. But wouldn't it be better if we took the buggy. It has a roof and so——'

'How long did you rent it for?'

'I paid just for the day. But Mr Grout said if I needed it for any longer, I could pay him when——'

Steele cut in: 'I don't want to take anything that's not mine.'

'But they're Albert's clothes, aren't they?'

He nodded. 'Be right back.'

He moved to the barn and was inside for perhaps half a minute. Returned with just a single item of clothing, which he had not taken in with him. When he climbed up beside her, he handed her a rain slicker similar to his own.

'Your brother's, Ruth. From his bedroll. Anything like that, taken between members of a family, is borrowing, I reckon?'

'Yes,' she agreed. He helped her put on the oilskin, then started the horse moving as she asked: 'The rest of Albert's clothing?'

'Scattered around the barn. It'll take him a little time to find it all and be ready to ride.'

'And that's what he'll do, Adam. Just as soon as he's able. He'll come after us. Albert isn't the kind of man who gives up on anything until it's finished or he knows for a fact it's a lost cause.'

'I don't doubt it, Ruth,' Steele rasped through gritted teeth as he struggled against an impulse to look back. 'After he's already put so much time and effort into finding me, it figures he's not going to throw in his hand now. And knowing you're with me, that'll strengthen his determination to see this through to the end?'

'I'm afraid so, Adam. Albert has always set great store by family ties.'

'There's nothing wrong with that, Ruth.'

'I know. But perhaps it would have been better if I didn't come with you?'

'Quit thinking that way, Ruth,' he told her as they approached the gate under the timber arch bearing the name of the spread, saw that Al Strachen had taken the trouble to re-fasten the gate when he returned from Broadwater.

'But——'

'But nothing,' he broke in, and showed a mirthless grin that could not be seen in the rain filled darkness as he brought the gelding to a halt. 'Even if family ties weren't involved, I'd still be in the same kind of bind.'

7

There was no further talk until they got to where the Timber Creek spur forked off the main trail and crossed the deeper-than-usual ford of the rain-swollen Providence River, and Steele steered the rig into a left turn, to head north. Then Ruth ended the silence that had existed since the wagon restarted after the Virginian closed the gate under the arch at the entrance to Trail's End.

'I should have realised you wouldn't go to town, Adam.'

He could not discern anything in her tone. And in the darkness of the rainy night he saw her face as no more than a pale shape, too indistinct to read her expression.

'Is there something in Providence you need, Ruth?' he asked, not liking the anxiety with which he hung on her answer.

'My bags. The clothes in them, but they aren't important.' She raised both her hands to display the purse they clutched. 'Fortunately, I make it a habit never to leave money in hotel or boarding house rooms.'

Now he tried not to reveal the relief he felt at the revelation that Ruth carried some travelling money. And suppressed the impulse to comment that he wished he had not made it a habit to stash most of his spare cash in the First Providence Town Bank: kept no money at the house and carried just a token emergency stake with him.

'That's good,' was all he said.

After a briefer pause than before, she asked: 'Do you have somewhere definite in mind to go, Adam?'

At the house, he had told her only that he was not going to turn himself over to the law. And that the single alternative to doing this was to leave Trail's End as quickly as possible, get to a place of safety where there would be time and opportunity to consider his plans for the future without pressing need to make hasty decisions.

'Broadwater, first stop,' he told her.

'Whatever you say, Adam.'

Perhaps a half minute elapsed before she wanted to know: 'Do you have friends you can trust in Broadwater?'

Now he had to quell an impulse to tell the woman angrily to shut up bothering him with questions. That in the second it had taken her to light the lamp in the barn, he had seen his entire life alter more dramatically than ever before: and he had been forced to make plenty of radical twists and turns in the past. That now he was out of imminent danger of his life coming to a sudden end—the teeming rain acting to erase the tracks of hoofprints and wheelrims from the trail—he needed a period of peace and quiet in which to come to some kind of terms with the traumas of the day.

But he realised in time that she did not deserve to be on the receiving end of his anger. And at a selfish level it would be self-defeating to alienate Ruth Blair. This woman who was the single good thing that had happened to him among the mass of evil: her support given selflessly, at a cost of considerable anguish. Support he had found almost over-whelmingly indispensable at that moment back in the house when he was on the point of leaving without her.

'No, Ruth,' he replied evenly. 'There's nobody I'd call a friend in that town. But Broadwater's a good place to hide in for awhile.'

'I'm sorry.'

'For what?'

'I've been badgering you, Adam. That's just as bad as nagging. Or prattling. I don't mean to do it.'

'But you have a need to talk?'

'I've never been one to brood, Adam. When I'm troubled, it seems to help to——'

'It's ten miles to Broadwater, Ruth,' he cut in. 'And it'll maybe seem like more in this weather. Which is pretty damn depressing even if everything else about tonight wasn't, uh?'

'That's true enough.'

'You could talk about you and your brother, Ruth.'

'Albert and me? What about us?'

'You know something of my murky past from talking to him, I reckon? I don't know anything about you. Except you're a recent widow, without too much reason to grieve. And you came to my place looking for your brother I didn't know was a United States marshal.'

'Well... Yes, that's right. It was certainly a strange co— No, it wasn't really a coincidence, was it?' Her tone was reflective, then morose. 'A twist of fate, I suppose: the way you and I... While Albert was...'

Steele said: 'If it's going to tie you up in knots, Ruth, maybe it'll be better to wait until later? When you can think straight, after you're not so mixed up about all that's happened so fast?'

'No,' she countered firmly, and curled a hand around his right forearm, gave it an affectionate squeeze. 'No, I'll only dwell on the misery of what's happened. And that won't serve any purpose whatever.'

She took a few moments to organise her thoughts, then fastened on a starting point: 'Albert and I have always been very close. He's seven years younger than me, and when we were children I used to mother him, I suppose. Which he never seemed to mind.

'The older we got, the closer we became. Then, when father died, it seemed our roles became reversed. Albert was the man of the house. He took over many of the duties of a husband. And father, too. And I'm afraid mother, who had loved our father as dearly as any woman can love a man, came to rely rather too much on Albert.

'He didn't have much of a life from when he was twelve and father died until he was twenty, when mother went. But he never seemed to mind. At first he was always lost in his studies, then he threw himself into the work he loved.'

Against the regular cadence of the rain hissing down on the timbered country and the almost unvarying sounds of the slow-moving horse and wagon, Ruth Blair's tone matched the subjects of which she spoke. She had loved her father, still admired her brother, resented the way her mother had taken advantage of Albert.

'Father had been a lawyer and from a young boy, Albert always wanted to follow in his footsteps. But he never had the ability. He worked so hard, but he failed to obtain the qualifications. So he got himself a job as a peace officer, which he thought was the next best thing. And proceeded to work himself up from being a constable in Philadelphia to a Pennsylvania marshal. Then to United States marshal.

'Mother hated for him to work. She would rather he stay in the house all the time. And there was no financial need for him to work, since father had left us quite well provided for. But much as Albert loved mother, he also loved the line of work he was in.

'Albert had always been her favourite and since I was at home all the time instead of him, I naturally bore the brunt of her disgruntlement.'

She paused, but there had been nothing in her tone to suggest she expected Steele to interject a comment. And after a few moments she vented a soft sigh, a sound like the final remnants of an inner anger she had felt over a long ago wrong. She went on:

'I never knew Albert cared about that—cared about much of anything outside of his precious upholding of the law—until mother died. Albert was away chasing criminals and he almost missed her funeral. It was after the burial he told me how much he appreciated what I'd done for him. By keeping mother from coming between him and his lawman's job. And he promised that he'd always look out for me. Come running if ever I needed his help.'

Once more she broke off and again there was nothing in her attitude that invited Steele to say anything. But he asked:

'He was twenty then and you were twenty seven? He wasn't a US marshal back then?'

'Yes, that's right. He was still a Phildelphia city constable.' She was starting to sound tired. But whether she was physically weary or jaded by past memories it was difficult to decide. 'But from a small boy, Albert always acted older than his years. And he acted it convincingly. He meant what he said. But I was determined not to trouble him with domestic problems. He'd had his fill of those while mother was alive.

'And I hardly saw him for the next three years. Then I met Eversly Blair and consented to marry him. Albert didn't like Eversly from the instant he saw him. He had a bad feeling

67

about him, he said. And he used every way open to him as a state marshal to delve into Eversly's past background. But he could not find that he'd done anything directly against the law. Just sailed close to the wind in his business dealings on occasion.

'And invariably finished up broke at the end of the day. Which made Albert think money was the reason Eversly wanted to marry me. And it's true that although we were not rich, Albert and I were neither of us poor. Since mother had lived very modestly on what father left.

'Anyway, I was thirty by then. And an unmarried woman of thirty has some bleak visions of what the lonely future holds, Adam. But regardless of that, I was convinced I was in love with Eversly Blair and just as certain he loved me as dearly. And I resented what Albert had done, checking up on Eversly that way. I suppose to some extent I still regarded him as my kid brother who had no business interfering with my private life. What he said about how he felt toward Eversly only strengthened my determination to marry. I can be pretty hard nosed and headstrong when I like.'

'That's no surprise, Ruth,' Steele said lightly.

She didn't respond for a few moments, then asked suddenly: 'I'm not boring you with this family history?'

'I asked you to tell it, Ruth,' he reminded her. 'And there's still the greater part of ten wet miles to Broadwater.'

'I'm trying to just tell the parts that show what kind of man my brother is.'

'You're doing fine.'

'Very well. Now, where was I? Oh, yes. Albert came to the wedding. He gave me away. Albert's always been very good at hiding his true feelings when he thought it was necessary and Eversly was totally ignorant of what my brother felt about him. Until we went to the train to travel to Denver—Eversly was from there and had seen a shoe store in the city he was interested in buying.'

'With your money?'

'I'm getting to that,' she said, a little snappily. Which Steele put down to her tiredness. She moderated her tone and went on: 'Just before the train left the station, Albert asked if he could see Eversly alone. They were gone only for a minute, but when Eversly came back, he was shaking. With rage, he said, but I think he was afraid, also.

'At first he wouldn't tell me what my brother said to him. He sat in silence for several miles obviously brooding on it. Until I insisted he'd better tell me about it or it would ruin our honeymoon. Which was not a good way to start our marriage.

'So he told me Albert had warned him he'd better treat me right and keep true to me. That if he ever heard differently, he'd come and find Eversly. And depending upon how badly he'd mistreated me, he'd either maim him or kill him.

'Eversly knew he meant it. And so did I, Adam. So you appreciate why I was so sure Albert would never have harmed me if you'd left me back at the ranch. He regards me so highly, you see?'

'Yes, Ruth.'

'Albert never says anything he doesn't mean. Which was why I was so concerned for you after he said the warrant authorised dead or alive. And he didn't really care all that much, one way or the other.'

'You kept in touch with Strach—with your brother—while you were married?'

'First I'll answer that other question you asked, Adam,' she insisted. 'Yes, just before we were married, I had let Eversly persuade me to put up the money for the store in Denver. I was perfectly willing to do so, but after his talk at the Philadelphia train station with Albert, Eversly wouldn't hear of using my money. Except for a little as a down payment. The rest for the business and the house that went with it he got with a loan raised by mortgage.'

'Did he keep faith with you? Treat you right?'

He thought he knew the answer. It was just something to say, to let her know he was still paying attention to the mundane domestic details she was speaking about. Trivia to fill the uncomfortable travelling time and occupy minds which would otherwise be troubled by doubts. But he was wrong, for after a moment went by, she offered a qualified response:

'Eversly treated me well, Adam. But he had ambitions to be a high flyer. He was never cut out to be a shoe store clerk, even if he owned the business.'

Another brief pause, then she went on hurriedly before he could phrase another question: 'You asked about Albert and I keeping in touch. Not on a regular basis. We exchanged letters every now and then. And twice when he was engaged in court duty that brought him to Denver, he stopped by the house. But I always knew I could reach him by writing or wiring an address in Washington. Which is what I did when Eversly had the fatal heart attack.

'Albert telegraphed back he was just starting to finish up a job. In the town of Providence, California. And he'd come by Denver to see me when his work was finished.'

'But you decided not to wait?'

She sighed. 'Truth to tell, I'd long ago had my fill of Denver and the shoe store, the same as Eversly. And I'd never had the opportunity to gain any relief in the way he did. I certainly tired very quickly of playing the part of the grieving widow, which I was absolutely not.

'So I quickly sold up the business and the house along with every item of stock and stick of furniture. And took the trip by way of San Francisco to Providence. I knew there was always a chance I'd miss Albert. But if I did, I'd be able to catch up with him somewhere else. If I still wanted to.'

'Yeah,' Steele said, and hoped she did not recognise in his tone a sign that he was glad she was through with the account that he, after all, had invited her to give.

'You know how I got to Providence and found my way out to your home, Adam,' she went on earnestly. 'And please believe me: I knew nothing of the job that brought Albert to this part of the country. And when Lavinia Attwood told me he was acting as a hired hand on your ranch, I certainly had no idea it was part of some ploy to trap you.'

He told her evenly: 'Just about everything you've done bears you out, Ruth.'

'It should have been everything, Adam,' she answered morosely. 'But when Albert first told me what he's certain you did, well . . .'

Steele could feel her eyes peering at him through the rainy darkness. And sensed the incredulity in her gaze. But was it disbelief at how she had let herself be persuaded by her brother to accept Steele had committed such crimes? Or that she had shared a bed with this man and now was helping him to escape the law in the full knowledge he was a brutal murderer?

He continued to look directly ahead along the dark trail when he said: 'He must have had quite a jolt, seeing you playing at housewife at Trail's End?'

'That's a fact,' she replied, a little breathlessly. 'I heard him ride up, naturally. Saw him from the window before I went to the door and he saw me. After he got over the shock, he told me he knew somebody else was on the place, because of the rented buggy on the yard.

'Then he became all lawman, Adam. Asked me where you were. And why I'd started to cook supper. I told him you were busy with a chore and since I had nothing to do except wait for him, I'd cook supper for the two of you.

'I didn't tell him anything about ... Well, you know: us doing what we did? And I know Albert would never suspect anything like that had happened so soon after we met. He's always been rather naive about men and women ... in that way. Obviously he knows about such relationships. But he's never had a ladyfriend to my knowledge. Or even been with a who—a woman—as far as I know. But that is neither here nor there.

'He told me you were the murderer he'd come to California to arrest. Bring back to Tennessee to stand trial. He went into all the details, because I told him right off I couldn't believe anything that bad about such a fine gentleman as you. And that made him terribly angry.

'After awhile I didn't listen too closely to what he told me. And I can't remember too much of what he said. Except you took the law into your own hands after your father was murdered. One by one you killed the men who had a hand in killing him. And when the lawman sworn to arrest you for your crimes caught up with you, you did for him, too.'

He filled the expectant pause she left. 'He tell you Bish was my best friend before the war, Ruth?'

'Yes, Albert told me so. James Bishop, that's one of the names I remember. I can't recall any of the others.'

'Reckon I could. If I were put to the test.'

'But it would serve no purpose?'

'I don't think so.'

'Albert was correct in everything he said, Adam?'

'If he told you those bare facts, Ruth: yes, he was right. They lynched my Pa.' He curled a hand to the Colt Hartford that rested across his lap, held there by his elbows.

'I read the inscription on the rifle, Adam. Albert showed it to me before he hid the gun away. I know Abraham Lincoln presented it to your father, Benjamin Steele, for services rendered. You want to tell me about it?'

'Whatever I tell you won't excuse what I did, Ruth.'

'I'm not asking for an excuse, Adam. Albert just told me the facts that he knew of what happened all those years ago. It wasn't his job to explain them. But if you want to ... Well, I guess we aren't yet even halfway to covering the ten miles to Broadwater?'

'Sure,' Steele said, and began to give Ruth Blair an unembroidered account of the violent events in which he became involved in the immediate aftermath of the War Between the States.

The pleasure he experienced at getting the letter from his father, who had supported the Union Cause, which offered reconciliation with his son, a former Rebel cavalry officer.

The horror in the Washington bar room where Benjamin P. Steele died. Right across the street from Ford's Theatre that same night they assassinated the President of the United States.

The feeling of desolation when he first saw the burned-down mansion amid the scorched fields of the once fine plantation.

The angry ride from Virginia into Tennessee, finding and killing the killers of his father with that special brand of cold-blooded lack of compunction he had learned about and honed during the war.

Killing Bish.

The remorseful, aimless trek that had taken him over the border into Mexico. Where, for day after day, he was sunk into a drunken stupor which failed to erase the memory of throttling his best friend to evade trial and punishment for his acts of retribution.

72

After he was through, and Ruth acknowledged it with another squeeze of his arm, there was a long time still left until they reached Broadwater. But by tacit common consent they agreed to finish the journey in silence: physically close together but alone in separate worlds of private reflections.

For his part, Steele was relieved by this arrangement. Because the events of this night and the constant struggle to suppress concerns about the days that were to follow had seemed to drain him of all but a final emergency reserve of energy: left him weary enough to have handed over the reins to Ruth if he believed she were capable of taking them with any degree of competence to handle the horse and wagon in her present condition.

But her physical contact with him was no longer confined to the light grip of her hand on his arm. She had started to sag heavily against his side. And her head often dropped to his shoulder. At first she jerked it up several times, but at length it lay there and he judged she had given in to the same kind of nervous exhaustion he had to struggle against.

After awhile, he held the reins in one hand and curled an arm around the woman to keep her from falling if the wagon wheels jolted into any deep ruts.

She sighed and nestled closer to him, murmured sleepily: 'I'm sorry, Adam. I know I should . . . But I feel so . . . so . . .'

Then she was asleep, breathing deeply and regularly, oblivious to what he said when he told her as he took a firm grip around her shoulders, recalling the sensations of touching her naked flesh:

'Ruth, to me you feel wonderful.'

The rain had slackened off to an irritating drizzle when the wagon rolled out of the timber below the crest of a hill from where there was an extensive view of Broadwater, stretching for a mile and a quarter along the eastern shoreline of the lake for which the town was named.

It was still early by Broadwater standards: at least, the standards of the pleasure palaces along the eastern side of Front Street across from the curving line of the narrow shingle beach, one of the town's three north to south thoroughfares. And except for occasional darkened business premises which did not operate on the axiom that a fool and his money are soon parted, almost every building on Front Street had brighly lighted windows, many of them reflected on the surface of the lake.

California Avenue, which ignored the contours of the lake side and was an arrow-straight extension of the trail from Providence, became an open trail again at its northern end, showed fewer lights. The ordinary working people of the town lived at its southern end, and at the far end California was flanked by mansions where Broadwater's rich, mainly elderly element resided. And either the need to rise early to face the rigors of a new day, or the aging process that calls for more than the average hours of sleep, caused the people in their humble houses or lavish mansions on California Avenue to bed down early.

Pacific Avenue, to where Steele made his way via one of the many narrow cross streets, was as straight as California. It ran at the base of the towering high ground which crowded Broadwater from the east, forcing the community to be much longer than it was wide.

Far fewer lights showed along Pacific than elsewhere in

town. And most of those windows which did gleam in the night from which the rain had now gone, had the tell-tale flicker of candlelight. Few people who lived along Pacific could afford the luxury of lamps and the kerosene or coal oil to fuel them.

This was the street of has-beens, total failures, optimists who hoped to make it and wishful thinkers biding their time between attempts to succeed. Some were permanent citizens of Broadwater and lived in one-roomed hovels. Most were transients, paying rent on rooms in hovels that were built two or three stories high which called themselves boarding houses or hotels. Often these larger places had exotic names painted on their ramshackle façades.

The Tivoli Hotel was up near the northern end of the street, on the corner of Eleventh. The Virginian went there with the upright and slow-walking but almost comotose Ruth Blair after he had parked the wagon on a vacant lot and had ensured that his gelding was bedded down in a livery with clean straw, fresh water and sufficient feed.

He knew nothing of the hotel: chose it simply because it was the closest place to the livery still open, and it was at the north end of town, almost as far as it was possible to get from Trail's End and Al Strachen without leaving Broadwater for open country.

A clock in the rancid-smelling lobby of the Tivoli started to strike midnight as he completed the scant formalities of checking in. He signed the stained and dogeared register as Mr and Mrs Wright. Watched by the proprietor who was very elderly, toothless and seemed to have no flesh between the angular bone structure and heavily bristled skin of his face, and a bleak look in his sunken eyes that suggested there was nothing in creation that could surprise him.

The wizened old man gave them directions and left them to their own devices to climb the creaking stairway and go along the unlit landing to a double room at the front of the narrow, three-story frame building that was even less imposing on the inside than its exterior.

Even as he had approached the hotel, Steele knew that had he been on his own, he would only have been able to afford a room in a place on Pacific Street. He was not alone, of course,

75

and Ruth had sufficient travelling money in her purse to afford better.

But there were three good reasons for not choosing a more comfortable place to stay the night. Perhaps of least importance in the circumstances was that it would go against his grain to call on Ruth for financial assistance until it was absolutely necessary. Also, he did not know how long their unequal joint stake would have to last, and it would be better to go easy with the money at the start. Most important of all, he was quite well known in some of the ritzier places on Front Street, and the last thing he needed was to be recognised.

Especially he did not want to be spotted by Sheriff Gavin Fenton, Luke Dexter or some other deputy. For as a United States marshal, Al Strachen would be required to make himself and his business known at the local office before he made a positive move in Fenton's jurisdiction.

Hell, Strachen may already have let the local lawman know he was hunting Adam Steele: sent a wire from the Providence telegraph office! He could have sent out the word to every law office in the damn state!

Steele had been in some tight corners down the years, but this one...

Just for a moment, as he followed Ruth up the stairs—ready to catch her if exhaustion overcame her and she fell back—he experienced regret at not leaving her on the spread. For if she were not with him, he would have detoured around Broadwater. Ridden as far as he was able away from his own territory. Bedded down as and when needed in whatever piece of cover presented itself at the time.

But Ruth was in desperate need of rest after the traumas of the evening. And it was better for her to have a rickety roof over her head and a lumpy mattress beneath her body than to camp out in the open this night. For although the rain had stopped, there was a threat of more to come from the sky, now blacked out by low, unmoving clouds.

When they reached the room, Steele lit the lamp on a low wick and began to explain his reasoning for bringing her to a place like this. But Ruth stopped him after a few moments, assured him it made no difference to her. She was out on her feet and the bed in the mouldy-smelling room looked

76

marvellous to her right then.

He did a double-take at her face, haggard with weariness, and realised then she would not even have noticed the unsavoury exterior of the hotel, the rancid smell in the lobby, the rickety state of the stairway, the dank landing and this squalid room furnished with just the bed and a chair.

She would have sunk gratefully down on the bed without taking off her wet clothing had he not stopped her: helped her to undress to her underthings without getting any erotic notions, while she remained impervious to modesty, false or otherwise.

Then he had her sit on the hard-seated, straight-backed chair while he stripped the bed of its covers, turned the mattress and remade it. No roaches or any other kind of bug dropped out.

She was asleep in a matter of seconds and he was sure it would be the same for him as soon as he lay down beside her. But first he needed to satisfy himself they had made it into the Tivoli without arousing any busybody interest.

He doused the lamp and checked Pacific and Eleventh Street from the two windows of the corner room that overlooked them. Saw no immediate signs of life in the vicinity of the hotel. And after a surveillance of several minutes he decided there were no surreptitious watchers hiding in dark doorways.

Then he left the room, moved silently to the top of the stairway and listened. Heard the old-timer bolt the front door. Then the lamp in the lobby was extinguished and the Tivoli's owner shuffled into his first floor living quarters.

Elsewhere, the only sounds in the hotel were of sodden roof timbers starting to dry out, a steady dripping of trapped rainwater finding a slow means of escape, and guests snoring.

He returned to the room and saw there was no lock or bolt on the door. So he wedged the chair under the knob, took off just his rain slicker and lay on top of the covers beside the sleeping woman.

Ruth continued to breathe deeply and regularly, wrapped in the recuperative sleep of the totally exhausted. Suffused by a brand of uncaring exhaustion that transcended the kind of nagging worries which would ordinarily not allow a mind to

77

be at ease while a body rested.

But as he listened to her against the silence of the building and its immediate surroundings, Steele soon realised that he would not so easily be able to sink down to the same level of sleep. For his mind would not let go of the constant barrage of regrets at how greatly his life had been changed since he went to sleep so contentedly—and complacently—in his own bed at Trail's End last night.

Too much of momentous importance had happened to him.

He was in danger of losing so much.

Or had he already lost everything that had mattered to him?

And suddenly the future was so uncertain that he felt like nothing short of a mammoth drinking jag would make him insensible to what had brought him to this squalid room in this stinking hotel with this wonderful woman: briefly end his concern for what was to happen to Ruth and himself when morning came.

That, or a crack over the head with something like the spade handle Ruth had used on her brother . . .

But that was a crazy way of thinking!

In Mexico, long ago, he had had his fill of drinking himself into fleeting oblivion. To try to forget the awesome event that had triggered so much, the long-ago event that had culminated in tonight when he opened the barn door and Ruth had lit the lamp.

When he emerged from that marathon drinking jag at the cantina in Nuevo Rio, all his troubles were still with him: especially the burden of remorseful guilt he felt for ending the life of Jim Bishop.

In later years he was to tell people that the month-long state of drunkenness had caused him to lose his taste for alcohol. But that was not true. Despite the quantity of cheap tequila he had poured down his throat, he had never lost his liking for the kind of top quality imported liquor he had been used to drinking back in Virginia.

What he had lost was any kind of liking for not being in control of what he was doing: and an awareness of what others were doing around him. For the style of life he drifted into when he rode north out of Nuevo Rio and back across the border demanded that he remain constantly alert to his surroundings. His survival had often depended upon it. And liquor did not make for sharp reactions.

Likewise, he had experienced on several occasions the kind of oblivion that comes with unconsciousness. And that was certainly not to be recommended as a substitute for good, deep, refreshing sleep.

He felt his bearded face form into the tight lines of an angry grimace. Only just managed to trap an obscenity into silence behind his gritted teeth.

What was he doing, thinking along these lines? In no circumstance was he going to get up from the bed, leave the room and the Tivoli Hotel to head away from this dark and sleeping section of Broadwater: go to the raucous, brightly-lit hotels, saloons, gambling joints and dance halls along Front Street.

To drink himself into an insensible stupor. Or start a fight that could get him a crack over the head. Get arrested in the end, maybe, and wind up in jail: emerge from self-inflicted oblivion with all his troubles still intact. Even multiplied manyfold from taking the crazy short term view: seeking what he knew never was the smart answer to anything.

But the hell with it!

While his mind was occupied with this futile line of thought, it was not free to go over and over what had happened to him earlier, was happening to him now and was likely to happen to him tomorrow.

The anger subsided and then he was forced to admit it had to be better to keep his real problems in mind. Consider constructive ways of handling them.

But when he tried to apply his mind to this exercise, it refused to obey him. Kept crowding with memories from the distant past: of the time when he had last been in danger for the same reason as now.

By contrast, he recalled, in those days of turmoil after the ending of the War Between the States, it had been easy for a man to escape justice by constantly moving on down the trail. Because then it had seemed like half the country was running away from one thing or another, and a man could get lost in the crowd, one fugitive among many.

Memories that got him nowhere . . .

Except asleep.

There was no intervening period of luxurious drifting between being in a troubled state of awareness and a deep, dreamless sleep. Suddenly he found the oblivion he wanted so desperately. Then he heard a voice softly call his name. Or was it shouted from a great distance away?

He snapped open his eyes to a strange quality of grey, somehow diffused light that filled the squalid room. Suppressed an urge to reach for the Colt Hartford. Rolled his head on the pillow and saw Ruth Blair looking over her shoulder at him from one of the windows, an anxious frown marring her beauty.

She was fully dressed except for the rain slicker. Had combed her hair, done her best to smooth out the creases the rain had made in her dress.

'Adam, you were starting to shout in your sleep,' she told him in low tones. 'A bad dream, I expect.'

'Uh?' He folded up on the bed. His head ached, he was goose bumped with cold and felt more tired than when he went to sleep. He remembered everything about yesterday.

'You were having a bad dream, Adam. And it could be dangerous. There are men down on the street. They're talking . . . In whispers, I guess. Like they don't want to be overheard.'

'How long have they been out there?' he asked.

He swung his feet to the floor and moved stiffly across to stand beside her at the window that overlooked Pacific Avenue. But there was nothing to be seen down there, because the strange light in the room was caused by a thick, impenetrable fog.

Down in the lobby, the longcase clock struck six times as the woman told him:

'I heard them first just a few minutes ago.'

She had cracked open the window and through the narrow gap came the barely audible sounds of voices and footfalls. Ruth was right. It was not only the muffling effect of the fog in the warming air of the newly-dawned day that gave the voices a secretive tone. The men were making efforts to whisper.

'What do you think? They do sound sort of——'

Steele shook his head sharply. Then he saw her crestfallen expression as she took the gesture as a criticism, and he hooked an arm around her shoulders. Pressed an index finger to the centre of his compressed lips as he leaned closer to the open window, head turned to place an ear to the gap.

'——this place, Sheriff. I'll check on it.'

'That's Albert!' Ruth murmured huskily.

Steele again nodded curtly, frowning as he recognised the voice of Gavin Fenton telling Strachen:

'That's the Tivoli, Marshal. Run by an ornery old buzzard named Clyde Barlow. Don't believe anything he tells you first off. And certainly don't let him talk you into paying hard cash for information he likely won't have anyway.'

'We're trapped in here, Adam,' Ruth hissed into Steele's ear that was not directed to the open window.

'Not until they know we're——' Steele started to correct as he blinked and rubbed his eyes with the heel of his free hand, trying to get better vision through the thick fog rolling in off the lake and along the streets of Broadwater.

He broke off what he was saying when he heard a bolt slide. Then the front door of the hotel creaked open and the emaciated old man Fenton had named as Clyde Barlow complained in whining tones:

'I heard what you said about me, Sheriff! And it's nothin' but a damn slander on me! I always speak the truth! Especially to the law!'

'I'd appreciate it if you'd keep your voice down, sir,' Strachen rasped softly, obviously having difficulty manufacturing politeness. 'I'm a United States marshal, looking for a man and a woman who——'

Steele heard no more because he turned and backed away from the window, steering Ruth ahead of him. He again pressed the forefinger of his free hand to his beard fringed lips when he saw the anxiety on her face and recognised she was about to pose a question.

He picked up the rain slickers from the floor, got the Colt

Hartford from where it leaned against the wall near the head of the bed on the side he had slept for what felt like just a few minutes but had been a couple of hours at least.

He withdrew his arm from around her shoulders and gave her Strachen's slicker. She put it on when she saw him don his own. Then he took the chair from under the door knob, started to ease the door open: inwardly cursing that he could not recall from last night if the hinges had creaked. Too many other factors of greater importance at the time had made this trivial. But this morning, with a United States marshal, the local sheriff and God knew how many deputies out on the streets in the vicinity of the Tivoli, the priorities were altered.

The creak of a dry hinge, or a loose floorboard, could make the difference between escape and capture. Ultimately, between life and death.

No, not ultimately, he corrected himself grimly as he pulled the door open silently until the gap was wide enough for him to pass through. If the showdown with the law was to be here and now, then it was here and now his fate would be decided. And he had no intention to be taken alive.

As he led Ruth by the hand along the landing, he heard the voice from below more clearly. For the stairway acted as a kind of sound chimney, drawing the exchange upward from the lobby.

'... give a damn if you're the Lord God Almighty himself, mister!' Barlow argued fiercely. 'You got no right to shove your way into my place and try to push an old man around!'

Steele, the frame of the Colt Hartford grasped tightly in his right hand, Ruth's wrist held more loosely in his left, moved gingerly along the landing toward the head of the stairway at the far end. Drawing closer to where he and Ruth would be visible to anyone in the lobby who happened to glance up the stairs. But closer, also, to a window that he knew from the geography of the building must look down from the rear of the Tivoli.

'That's not what I'm here to do, sir,' Strachen was saying, his voice getting tenser with the strain of controlling his irritation with the old man he had been warned was difficult. 'I just have to ask you a question. And depending how you answer, I may wish to step inside and question one of your guests. But first, Mr Barlow, I'd ask you to keep your voice down, sir. In the event you alert——'

'Okay, ask away, young man,' the old-timer broke in impatiently.

Ruth stiffened, as she had earlier in the room when she had first heard her brother's voice.

Steele halted and let go of her wrist. Had no need to emphasise the need for silence again as he held the Colt Hartford out toward her. She looked afraid to touch it, until he showed her a fleeting smile.

She accepted it with a soundless gulp and he stepped across the head of the stairs. Glanced down as he did so. Saw tendrils of fog, smelling damp but fresh against the mildewed odours of the hotel, wisping into the lobby. Glimpsed a back view of the full length of Clyde Barlow's slight frame inside the threshold. Saw Al Strachen only from the waist down, standing out on the street. The marshal wore a sheepskin jacket, rucked up on the right to display the butt of a Colt revolver jutting out of his tied-down holster.

Then Steele was in an alcove beyond the point where the stairs reached the landing: the door to a closet on his right, the blank wall of the room across from the top of the stairs to his left.

A man was snoring regularly within the room, enjoying a deep and untroubled sleep. On the far side of the door to the room, Ruth stood in an attitude of rigid tension, her knuckles white from the tightness of her grip on the Virginian's rifle. She seemed oblivious to Steele as she stared fixedly at the head of the stairway, hearing the voice of her brother from little more than fifty feet away.

The window was uncurtained, except by dusty cobwebs. But even when Steele brushed away some of the dirt with a gloved hand, he saw that the scene outside was totally blanketed by the grey fog. He did not need to do any cleaning off of dirt to see that the window could not be opened without a lot of noise. For long ago when Clyde Barlow or his predecessors had taken the trouble to lavish a little care on the Tivoli, the window frame and its jamb had been painted many times. But the painters had never opened the window, nor removed earlier coats of paint. Thus, the window was effectively sealed closed by several layers of brown paint.

Down on the threshold of the Tivoli, Strachen had asked Barlow if a man named Adam Steele was staying at the hotel. With a woman named Ruth Blair, or maybe Ruth Strachen. The old man had replied that nobody with those names had rooms in his place. Last night or any other night that he could remember. Then, as Steele reached a decision about the window, the marshal said:

'They could have used different names, sir. Bogus names. It's likely they did. So if you——'

'Well, how in hell am I supposed to figure out folks that come to the Tivoli ain't usin' the names they were born with?'

Strachen pressed: 'The woman's blonde. Pushing forty. The man has a grey beard and is ten years or so——'

'Hey, Marshal!' a man yelled from south of Pacific Avenue. 'There's a flatbed over here where it shouldn't be. You say they took off on a wagon like that?'

'Wake the whole damn town, why don't you, Delany!' Gavin Fenton bellowed.

Knowing there was no longer any purpose to be served by keeping his voice down in this area, Al Strachen roared: 'I'm coming!' But lowered his voice as he turned away from the hotel entrance, told Barlow: 'Maybe I'll be back in awhile, sir.'

Running footfalls thudded on the street as the searchers converged on the weed-choked vacant lot where Steele had left the wagon, a hundred yards down from the hotel on the other side of Pacific Avenue.

Barlow crashed the door angrily closed, muttered that he thought everyone was supposed to keep their voices down, then shuffled across the uncarpeted lobby and began to climb the stairs.

He uttered an occasional groan, like the effort of lifting one foot ahead of the other triggered rheumatic pains. Came to a grimacing halt when he sensed he was being watched from above. Looked in that direction to direct a watery-eyed gaze at Steele who had swung into sight on the landing.

Barlow was startled for just a moment, then recovered and accused sourly: 'Your name ain't Wright!'

'It's always suited me fine,' Steele answered evenly as Ruth stepped forward to stand beside him. He took the Colt Hartford from her, sloped the barrel to his shoulder while he fisted one hand around the frame, in the way that he generally carried the rifle.

Barlow snorted, then challenged: 'Seems to me there ain't no time to waste foolin' around with words!'

The man in the room at the top of the stairs continued to snore rhythmically as Steele agreed lightly: 'Reckon that is right, Mr Barlow.'

'Okay, keep it up long as you want!' the old man wearing a threadbare topcoat draped over a grubby nightshirt growled. 'But I figure it'll be smarter if you pay me ... Let's say, a month's rate for the night you stayed at the Tivoli? And I won't say nothin' to any lawmen about how you and the lady were——'

'That seems like a high price to pay, feller,' Steele broke in as the street became silent, the sleeping man's snores sounded louder by contrast.

'Don't trust him, Adam!' Ruth warned nervously, and rested a hand gently on Steele's forearm.

'Well, it's said that silence is golden, ain't it?' Barlow asked rhetorically. He cackled with brief laughter, then was earnest as he went on: 'But I ain't that fussy. I'll sell mine for treasury bills, mister whatever your name is?'

Steele vented a low, non-commital groan and swung the rifle down from his shoulder.

Ruth gasped.

The toothless old man with eyes that had seen so much over a long life showed a gummy, bleak smile as he claimed: 'I'm ninety two years old, mister. Seem to recall I got over my fear of passin' on to a better place when I was about eighty five or so. So threats don't wash with me no more. Just interested in money. Make the time I got left to me more comfortable. Pay for the fine funeral I've got planned.'

'Don't reckon to scare you, old-timer,' Steele drawled.

He moved the rifle with slow deliberation, ensured the barrel never dipped to aim at Barlow.

'You better not. Like I say, it won't wash. Just the thirty bucks is what interests me. Then I won't tell the local sheriff and that out-of-town marshal you and lady are here. Until I maybe remember a couple looked like you stayed here. By which time you'll be pretty far away? We got us a deal?'

Steele side stepped. With a violent thrusting movement cracked the stock of the rifle against the dusty pane of glass in the paint-sealed window. And in the confined space it seemed like the crash of breaking glass sounded as shockingly loud as if he had triggered a shot to send the frail old man tumbling down the lower half of the stairway.

Ruth was able to partially trap a shriek of alarm in her throat, so that it emerged as no more than a strangled squeak.

Barlow was startled for just a second. Then his emaciated face formed into a scowl and he complained bitterly: 'I'd have kept my part of the bargain, damnit!'

Steele growled: 'I didn't want to put you to any trouble, feller.'

'You're crazy if you think you can get away from Gavin Fenton!' Barlow snarled. 'This town's got the best lawman in the state of California! You ain't got no——'

'What the frig's happenin' out there?' the rudely-awakened man in the nearby room demanded. 'What was that crash?'

Steele growled against a distant chorus of raised voices out on the street: 'I broke a window. Now I've got to shatter an illusion.'

9

Steele swept the barrel of the rifle around the window frame, knocked out the shards of glass that were still held by putty which was a lot less secure than the paint that glued the window shut.

Then he whirled away from the impenetrable morning air that streamed in through the window to press the dampness of Lake Providence against his skin.

'You gotta be a crazy man,' Barlow said croakily from halfway up the stairs.

Ruth murmured breathlessly: 'I have to admit I'm thinking much the same, Adam.'

Barlow complained more forcefully: 'It costs money to get a busted window fixed!'

'Take care of this again,' Steele instructed. He thrust the rifle at the woman and she instinctively took it, fisted her hands around the barrel and the frame.

'Adam?' she pleaded, taut with fear.

He swung away from her, raised a leg over the ledge and ducked his head through the frame of the window, said: 'If he tries to stop us, hit him with it.'

He started to manoeuvre himself out of the window, into a position to lower himself to the ground, which he knew should be one story down.

'I don't——' she started to tell him. And her tone and expression conveyed she had maybe had her fill of taking violent action when she knocked out her brother with the spade handle.

'Okay, okay!' the old man blurted. 'I'm gonna go!'

His tread sounded heavily on the stairway. Then his voice was a snarl as he yelled up at the woman from a safe distance: 'But I'll tell 'em! I'll tell them lawmen you and him was here!

Miss or Mrs or whatever you are!'

Steele's leading foot crunched on broken glass a short distance below the window. He was briefly disconcerted as he felt hurriedly around with the foot, then grinned back into the building as he drew his other leg up and stepped outside, enveloped in the fog that reduced visability to just a couple of feet.

'Adam?' Ruth asked, looking and sounding helpless: at a loss to understand his sudden change of expression as he stooped to peer in at her, reached toward her with both hands.

'Give me the rifle and come on out,' he told her. 'It's a flat roof of the next door building.'

She hesitated for a second or so. And as he peered at the anxious frown on her face, saw a tremor go through her body, he was worried she had endured too much for the wife of a shoe store owner, now the companion of a fugitive.

'I'll tell Gavin Fenton and that marshal right now, I will!' Clyde Barlow yelled vehemently up the stairway. 'And I don't give a shit what kinda crime you got to pay for! You'll sure pay for bustin' my window, I'll see to that!'

'Quit all this damn noise in the middle of the friggin' night!' the newly-awakened man bellowed, his rage as great as that of Barlow.

It was like the sounds of the men's angry voices were what Ruth needed to spark her into action, impel her further down the road of helping Steele escape the consequences of the ancient crime.

'Yes,' she decided in a rasping whisper.

Then she tried to push the rifle toward Steele. But the stock jammed against one side of the window frame, the barrel the other. And she mouthed something he thought was one of the less obscene profanities.

He took the rifle from her grasp, pulled it through the window. She hurried to climb out after it: trusting him but shaking her head to refuse his offer to help her.

'You lead and I'll follow, Adam,' she promised. 'And I think the quicker we get started, the better it'll be for us.'

Because they were at the rear of the hotel, on the flat roof of the single-story building next to the Tivoli on Eleventh Street, the shouting voices on Pacific were now not only distorted by the muffling effect of the fog, but also by the intervening bulk of the hotel.

And there was plenty of shouting, accompanied by running footfalls, as the posse of lawmen hurried down the street from where Steele had abandoned the flatbed wagon, drawn by the frantic yells of Clyde Barlow letting it be known the hunted couple were escaping from his place.

Steele spent just a few moments trying to recall what kind of building was beneath his feet. Was it a house or a store? If a store, had it looked like there were living quarters out back?

But it was obvious the memory was not going to be released and, like Ruth had said, it was important to get away from the Tivoli as soon as possible. If there were occupants within the building beneath them, they would surely have already been roused out of sleep by all the noise.

It was still to their advantage to move as quietly as possible, though. And as soon as Ruth was out of the window beside him, he grasped her hand. And, using the rifle in the way a blind man uses a cane, he led the woman toward the front of the building on Eleventh Street. In the thick fog, he preferred the open street to a maze of back alleys or cluttered rear yards that were likely to be the alternative. Some of the yards were patrolled by dogs which he could hear contributing barks and snarls and whines to the human cacophony from Pacific Avenue and from the stairway and landing of the hotel.

He set down his feet as lightly as he could and Ruth took her cue from him: understood there was a possibility that people had been awakened in the building underneath them, would plunge outside and add their voices to the hue and cry if they heard movement on the roof. But the fog-shrouded area immediately around and beneath Steele and the woman remained so quiet that every sound they made seemed disproportionately loud to their own ears.

Then the gently prodding rifle stabbed thin air below the level where it had previously touched the pitch covered roof.

Steele halted and Ruth vented a soft gasp as she came to a halt herself, afraid something was wrong.

Voices sounded more loudly as some of the men headed for the corner of Eleventh Street, surely drawn there by being told that Steele had smashed a window to make his escape on this side of the Tivoli. Other voices were raised and heavy footfalls could be heard crashing on the stairway and along the landing in the hotel.

A man roared in high excitement: 'Hey, you guys! They got out this way! Shit!'

'What's wrong?' Gavin Fenton demanded within the hotel.

'Cut my friggin' hand on busted glass!'

He got no sympathy that carried out to the pair on the roof as Steele released Ruth's hand, immediately curled an arm around her waist. She snapped her head around to look apprehensively at him. He gestured with his head that they were going to launch themselves off the front of the roof: plunge through the curtain of fog.

She shook her head sharply and her eyes grew wide with terror of the unseen, the unknown.

He pushed his faced close to hers, murmured softly: 'It's a chance of breaking a leg against getting my neck stretched, Ruth. A risk I have to take. Count of three.'

She seemed not to trust herself to speak.

'One,' he whispered. Continued to peer at her while he withdrew his arm from her waist, to signal he was willing to leave her here on the roof if that was what she wanted.

'Two?' His tone was questioning.

She gave an emphatic nod of agreement. Clutched at his hand as he swung his head around to face front and down.

'Three.'

'Yes.'

He launched himself off the roof and she went at the same instant: every muscle in their bodies tensed for crunching impact with the unseen street—or whatever bone breaking obstruction was on the street.

Steele felt like he was leaping off a high cliff with his eyes closed. The stretched second while he dropped through impenetrable thin air seemed to be elongated to many. And in that time it was compelling to give in to the kind of fear of the unknown that triggered shrieking vocal outlet.

But neither he nor Ruth made a sound until, feet first, they slammed into the street. Which, although it had been softened by last night's teeming rain, was still less than resilient beneath them.

She snatched her hand free of his grasp and he surrendered it gratefully. For they both needed to flail their arms in an effort to maintain their balance. Or to break their fall if the momentum of the leap pitched them to the muddy ground.

Steele took three staggering steps on painfully jarred legs before he could be sure he was going to stay on his stinging feet. He could not see Ruth, but he thought he heard her utter a squeal, although whether the sound was one of pain, alarm or relief he could not tell before a chorus of voices bellowed louder than before. And some of what was said could be discerned against the general ruckus:

'What was that?' 'I thought I heard somebody——' 'I don't friggin' know!' 'Shit, it sounded like——'

Then, closer than the rest: 'What the frig . . . Gee, I'm sorry, ma'am, but——'

'Adam!'

Ruth's voice was shrill with a greater degree of fear than he had seen in her eyes when she realised they were going to jump off the roof. And in a moment it had acted to still the competing voices on the stretch of street where Steele came to a momentary halt. Before he whirled to the side. Lunged in the direction from which Ruth had shrieked her plea for help.

'Hot damn, you must be the one——'

The man whose surprise turned to triumph had his back to Steele. A shadowy form in the fog, facing an even more indistinct figure: surely Ruth Blair.

'Ad——' she started to yell for Steele again. Just as the man she had collided with in the fog brought up both his hands toward her, a laugh exploding from his throat.

Then, as terror caused Ruth's voice to fail her, the man about to grab her either realised she was not alone, or sensed an imminent threat. Whichever, he silenced the laugh and whirled away from the woman.

Steele had jerked up the rifle by then, was swinging it. Took a backward step to place the man's head in line with the arc of the heavy stock.

The man was turning so his face was toward the rifle become a club, and it was the bridge of his nose that took the forceful thud of rosewood. And the crunch of fragmenting bone masked whatever cry of pain emerged from his gaping mouth, as he crumpled to the ground like a loosely-filled sack, unconscious an instant after the blow struck his face and split the skin to release a gout of crimson.

Steele did not recognise the man from the fleeting glimpse he got of him.

'Adam!' Ruth forced out of her constricted throat as she plunged toward him.

Many voices were raised again. And once more, much of what was yelled was indistinct. But an occasional word sounded clearly enough to convey that other men were demanding to know what one of their number had found, and why he was not answering their questions.

'I thought——' Ruth blurted as Steele sloped the rifle to a shoulder and grasped her hand.

'Just keep thinking it's best we move fast,' he told her, and jerked her into a run.

For several paces he could only hope he had not lost his bearings during the clash with the man. Because now his only point of directional reference in the fog was the increasing volume of sound that signalled where most of the searchers were located.

This suddenly got louder than ever as the unconscious man was found slumped on the street: and irritation turned to raging anger in many voices as the men urged each other to increase their efforts at finding the couple who had done this to one of their own.

The noise masked the running, splashing footfalls of Steele and Ruth. And the woman's ragged, rasping breathing.

Steele knew as he plunged into the wall of fog that they were moving away from the men who hunted them. But not until they had covered several yards could he be sure they were racing blindly down the centre of Eleventh Street. Would not come to a painful halt as they smacked into the front of a building, or tripped on a raised sidewalk to pitch to the boarding with the same result.

He slowed to a walk, told her softly: 'All right, we can take it a little easier now, Ruth.'

'Adam, I——' she started, but was too breathless to go on.

'Just try to act as curious as anybody we bump into about all this ruckus,' he said. Was about to expand on this, but bit back on the words when a commanding voice rang out clearly above all the others back along the street.

'——said to be quiet, you people!'

It was Gavin Fenton who snarled the order, and as this began to be obeyed, Al Strachen complained in a kind of stage whisper:

'A herd of buffalo could stampede out of town under cover of ...'

His voice trailed away to an inaudible whisper as near silence enveloped the street. Disturbed by the barking of a lone dog. Then, when the animal quietened, the footfalls of Steele and Ruth were all the couple could hear. When they halted, the only sound to penetrate the seemingly solid barrier of the fog was the steady dripping of moisture off the eaves of buildings.

It was eerie in the stillness. And the wet air felt much colder than it actually could be this summer early morning.

'I'm sorry,' Ruth murmured, her lips close enough to brush Steele's ear.

He squeezed her hand and she was content with his acknowledgement. When he started slowly forward, she moved along at his side, matching her pace to his. Like a small child totally trusting the man who was leading her into the solid-looking but always retreating wall of fog.

Time continued to be stretched and for what seemed like much longer than it could have been, Steele continued to advance, his eyes never wavering in their unblinking gaze ahead while his hearing was attuned to pick up the first sound of a threat.

He had to make a conscious effort to keep a check on his imagination: not to believe that the hunters were closing in on all sides, drawn by the squelching footfalls and rapid breathing of the quarry. Also, there were siren voices in his head that he found difficult to ignore from time to time. Voices that tried to panic him into changing direction: screamed that he had turned without knowing it in the fog and was heading back toward the posse of lawmen.

Men who were only moments away from capturing him. And the woman: the only good thing still left in his life.

The newest and the best.

Ruth. Who, by helping him to escape, being right there when

he hit a man so hard with the rifle he may have killed him, was as guilty as Steele. And it did not matter that she was the sister of the United States marshal sworn to bring in Steele. Not when her brother was as dedicated to upholding the law as she had said he was.

Then Steele rid his mind of voices and the danger of panic they created. His entire way of life had been shattered in the time it took for a lamp to be lit. But he continued to exist and he had Ruth, who made living worthwhile now that everything else was gone. And he must keep his wits about him, protect her from the worst consequences of stepping across such a dangerous line.

He angled to the right, counted the steps he took and reached the sidewalk in fifteen. So, he estimated, he had been heading along the centre of Eleventh Street. But he had not thought to keep tally of how far he had moved away from the Tivoli Hotel on the corner of Pacific Avenue.

He could have led the trusting Ruth Blair across the intersection of California Avenue without being aware of it, in which event they were now closing with Front Street. On the other side of which was the shingle beach and the lake beyond.

'Adam?'

He started forward, the sidewalk immediately on his right. He was still unsure if he was approaching the corner of California Avenue or Front Street, hoped he sounded more confident than he felt when he assured her:

'It's all right, Ruth.'

'Good,' she said and sounded like she was convinced he was in full control of their situation. Until she qualified it: 'So long as you know where we're going.'

Which he did not: once they reached Front Street, however far away it was.

Then he heard something and caught a new smell in the cold, damp air that he knew ought to be familiar to him in this combination. And suddenly he had it!

'What's wrong?' Ruth asked as he came to a halt.

A spontaneous smile took over his bearded face as he had to make a conscious effort not to let relief sound in his voice when he told her: 'About another hundred yards and we'll be on Front Street, Ruth.'

'And?'

Now it was difficult not to feel irritated with her. But, he told himself sourly, it was a perfectly reasonable response to his bald statement after he recognised the bubbling sound of a great deal of boiling water and smelled the soapy steam it gave off. Knew the combination came from the Chinese laundry two streets north, on Fourteenth. And the laundry was between California and Front.

Then a solution to his immediate problem, and answer to her question, flashed into his head.

'Across Front Street is the lake.'

'And?'

There was fear implicit in the single word and he swung his head around to peer into her frowning face. Brightened his grin as he told her lightly:

'Don't plan to swim it.'

She did not respond, except by looking even more afraid.

He went on: 'There are some rowboats on the beach as I recall. Enough of them so one won't be missed when the fog lifts. Until the owner shows up to use it.'

Ruth told him tautly: 'Adam, I get sick in boats.'

A gunshot cracked. It was some way behind them, but they both instinctively ducked: Ruth from ignorance, Steele in no clear-thinking state of mind to remember from experience that somebody who gets shot doesn't hear the muzzle report until after the bullet strikes home.

There was no sound of this bullet thudding in anything solid close by as distant voices were raised, questioning and complaining.

Ruth uttered a small cry.

'Somebody shooting at a shadow,' Steele said, clutched her hand more tightly as he started forward more quickly than before. Not so much to widen the gap on their pursuers who were obviously in disarray, as from a sense of confidence at having gotten his bearings and formed a plan of sorts to shake off the posse.

'Nobody was ever killed by seasickness, I guess?' Ruth asked after a few paces. She was trying to suppress her fear by an effort of will, heard in the forced lightness of tone. 'Adam, I'm sorry for being such a——'

'We're both sorry for a whole lot, Ruth,' he broke in on her, his attempt to sound unconcerned sounding less strained. 'Maybe the lake can help us with that, too?'

'What? I——'

'We can try to toss them overboard, Ruth. I reckon the lake's deep enough to drown our sorrows.'

10

Because the sound of the hue and cry had been concentrated on the far side of Broadwater, and only the gunshot would have carried obtrusively to Front Street, the final few hundred feet of their escape from the Tivoli Hotel to Providence Lake was much less fraught with tension than at the start.

For Steele knew this town. Guessed that few of the people who lived along the lakeside street devoted to hell raising far into the night would be awake. Or even sleeping lightly enough to be disturbed by distant sounds.

But he could sense Ruth was still ill at ease: largely, he decided, at the prospect of having to get into a boat.

Across the broad width of the street, away from the close-packed buildings with their dripping eaves, in the stillness of a morning when there was no stirring of wind to ripple the lake and raise waves at its fringe, just one other sound apart from the crunching of their feet on the shingle could be heard. The occasional plaintive call of a curlew far out over the lake.

'That's a sad sound,' Ruth said, her tone melancholy to match her subject as they came to a halt.

'How sad are you, Ruth?'

'What?'

'At cutting yourself loose from the kind of life you've always led? Throwing in with a man who takes you to the cheapest hotel in town? Gets you out through a back window with a posse of lawmen hard on our——'

'Is this the time and place?' she asked, a sharp tone of criticism in her voice. Then she trembled as she snapped her head from side to side.

He didn't think she was cold. Chose to put the tremor down to thoughts of the imminent boat ride: rather than fear of being captured by the men hunting them.

Suddenly, he pulled her gently forward. It was plain she thought he was taking her into his arms to comfort her. And although she knew this was neither the time nor the place for this, either, she became compliant: even closed her eyes and readied her lips for a kiss.

But her eyes widened and her mouth fell open in surprise when her leading foot clunked against something solid. She looked down and saw a rowboat, leaning over on its side on the beach.

'Oh,' she murmured, and swallowed hard.

Steele gestured in the blanketing fog with the rifle, said: 'Providence Lake is more than three miles long and two wide at its widest, Ruth. I ride horses or drive a wagon. Walk sometimes, run not so much. Mostly I can see which way I'm going and have some idea of where I'm heading.'

From a distance, maybe closer than they sounded in the sound muffling fog, men shouted at each other. Just their voices, not the words, reached the beach.

'Adam, we must still move quickly.'

Steele nodded, stooped and started to drag the twelve-feet-long, clinker-built rowboat across the shingle. The slithering sound it made seemed very loud, but it did not have the penetrating shrillness of the men's voices.

Ruth moved to help him, then held back when the boat, smelling of old fish and with a pair of oars in the bottom, was floating: would have drifted away from the shore if Steele had not held on to a six-feet-long painter tied to the bow.

'I know,' he told her. 'But you have to know what you're letting yourself in for, Ruth. The only boats I've been on before were steamers on the Mississippi and Red Rivers. On those, I wasn't doing the navigating. And the weather was a whole lot better than this.'

'Talk is wasting time, Adam.'

The shouting had died down, but that did not inspire confidence. The silence acted to increase tension: encouraged minds to conjure up images of furtive figures advancing through the fog.

'This is the point of no return, Ruth,' Steele said quickly, his voice tense with the effort of whispering. 'Once we're out there in this weather I can only hope I'm heading in the right direction. Across the lake. Or up the lake. If I go wrong, I could head us out of the lake, into the Providence River.'

'Which will take us back where we started from, right?'

'It would, if there wasn't a canyon not too far downriver. Where the boat and we would be smashed to pieces in the rapids.'

'Or in this fog you could steer the boat around in a circle. Back to the shore. And Albert and his——'

'It could happen.'

'Or the fog could lift and anybody who happened to be on the shore would see us. And if we were close enough they could take shots at us?'

'Right.'

'They add up to a great many chances I'm prepared to take, Adam,' she told him earnestly. 'But, believe me, the worst one I'm taking is that I might get so sick to my stomach, I'll wish I was dead anyway. And while I'm wishing I were dead, I'll look like death. Which no woman wants. So, if this is the point of no return, Adam, let's get beyond it. Please?'

'Thanks, Ruth.'

'You don't want to hear I'm sorry. For being a woman who can slow down a man when he has to move fast. I don't want to hear you're a man ready and willing to admit that some times the presence of a woman can make things easier for him. Just let's get moving, Adam. But don't count on any help from me until I'm off this boat, wherever that happens to be.'

For the first time since they were at Trail's End—in bed, while he was out working on the spread, then riding back to the house expecting to sit down to a fine supper cooked by this woman—Steele felt almost recklessly happy. The kind of happiness that for long moments acted to transcend all else. While he felt an overwhelming compulsion to take her in his arms, tell her how much he was indebted to her for what she had said, all that was implicitly promised by it.

'Adam, there'll be time later,' she said, with a perception that signalled she had looked into his face, guessed what was in his mind.

He answered thickly: 'I just hope there are the words, Ruth.'

Then he hauled the bow of the boat back up on to the beach, helped her in and to get seated at the stern, facing the bow.

Then he shoved the craft fully into the water, tossed his rifle aboard and got his pants wet to the knees as he turned it around. Then he aligned the stern with the beach and almost capsized the boat when he climbed in over the gunwale.

Ruth Blair gave a small cry of fear as the boat tilted and then for a half minute or so he was too busy fitting the oars into the rowlocks and adjusting his stroke to set what he hoped was a straight course out into the centre of the lake to be aware of the woman.

When he found a smooth rhythm that he thought ought to maintain an unvarying course, he looked at Ruth. Saw her less clearly than at almost any time since they clambered out of the second story window of the Tivoli Hotel into the all-enveloping fog.

For out on the lake, the prime source of the dawn greyness, it was thicker than in town and Ruth was half a length of the boat away from him. He could just about make her out as she sat with her shoulders hunched, elbows on her knees, face dipped into her cupped hands.

'Ruth?'

'Adam, please don't,' she said thickly, liquid sounding in her throat. 'I think it's going to work.'

'What is?'

She continued to speak into her hands. 'All you told me about what could go wrong out here. I'm so scared of that, it's keeping my mind off . . . Oh! Please don't talk to me any more. Unless it's absolutely imperative?'

'All right.'

After maybe a minute of the silence she had requested, he decided this was the strangest time of all he had spent with this woman since he made his presence known to her at the corner of the barn while she stood in the centre of the yard at Trail's End.

But it was not silent, of course. There was a great deal of noise. The splashing of the oars into and out of the lake; the creaking of the rowlocks; his own deep breathing; the rippling of water along the boat's hull and the occasional melancholy call of the distant curlew.

No voices, though. That was what made it so weird. With the exception of short spans of dangerous time, it had only been while Ruth was sleeping and he tried to sleep in the squalid hotel room that talk had been missing between them.

He would sure like to have her talk to him now as he pulled on the oars: this act of rowing the boat into the unknown, his back to the way he was going, more disconcerting than hurrying along streets through the thick curtain of fog.

This was because being on the water was such an unfamiliar experience for him, he supposed.

Much as he felt drawn to peer over his shoulder, he knew it would be a mistake: for to turn his head and maybe his body could easily cause him to alter course. And what was there to see? The vast expanse of Providence Lake had no islands, nor even rocks that showed above the surface.

Which was good. There was nothing for the boat to collide with, so no need for Ruth to keep watch.

He suppressed the urge triggered by unreasoning fear to have her talk to him. She had her own private troubles as she sat hunched on the stern seat: was experiencing her own brand of unnerving demons as she fought to ignore the motion of the boat across the deep water by nurturing the less awesome fear of capture.

Time passed, its span elongated by the absence of talk and the way this intensified the other sounds which were so unfamiliar to him.

Which was a crazy way to think, he told himself under his breath. It was vital he keep a grip on reality: fasten his mind on those facts of which he could be certain. The lake was beneath him and the sky above. And provided he avoided rowing around in circles, the boat would eventually hit something. The western shore of Lake Providence, he hoped.

What then?

With Ruth Blair so deeply engrossed in controlling her urge to be sick, he asked the question of himself. Had to be truthful and admit he did not know.

He had successfully achieved two objectives. Reached Broadwater yesterday and Lake Providence this morning. Now there was no specific aim in his mind, except the general one of escaping immediate capture and ultimate punishment for the old killing.

Trail's End was gone, along with the entire comfortable way

of life that had come with the spread. Even the horse and wagon he had used to get to Broadwater had been abandoned. And all he could call his own were the clothes he wore, the Colt Hartford rifle and ... Yes, damnit, and the woman. Who had asked him not to rely upon her for anything until they were off the boat with dry land beneath her feet.

Which was fine.

Ruth was a welcome added bonus at the start of his return to the deprived life of a wanted man drifting where fancy took him or the law chased him. He could surely get along without her active support for awhile.

But soon ...

He became suddenly self-consciously aware of needing Ruth as more than a compliant body, a ready arm to lean on or even a shoulder to cry on. With all he had struggled for over so many years now taken from him, she was his only source of money.

He heard himself rasp a curse. Did a fast double-take at Ruth and was relieved to see that if she heard him, she was not going to interrupt the state of mind in which she could control her terror of being on the boat.

Not for the first time he held the oars above the lake surface, let the boat glide through the water with the momentum of earlier strokes. But now, instead of listening for sounds of pursuit, he swept his gaze the length of the boat: searching for Ruth's purse.

His mind filled with memories of all that had happened since he awoke to her calling his name, to tell him to stop shouting in his sleep because men were gathering outside. But he could not recall a time when he had seen her clasping the purse.

He quelled an impulse to call her name and ask the question. Then dipped the oars again, pulled harder than ever. Not wanting to add to her distress by reminding her of the lost money, but anxious to get ashore where the matter of the missing purse could be resolved, one way or the other.

Despite the fog that shrouded everything anyway, he squeezed his eyes tightly closed, to help to concentrate his entire being into the effort of driving the boat through the water as fast as possible. Was lost to his surroundings, in the same withdrawn state Ruth tried to create for the length of time he was unable to measure.

Then he was jerked out of this by a scraping sound and a sudden slowing of the boat. Moments later it came to a stop, but not hard enough to throw either of them off their seats. For the shore on which the boat had come to rest shelved as gently as the beach from which they had pushed off. And the forward motion of the boat carried it several feet on to the shingle after the total buoyancy of the water was lost, braked it to a halt without violence.

'What's happened?' Ruth asked fearfully. Her face was drained of colour when she jerked her hands away, snapped her head around to look in all directions, lastly short-sightedly at Steele.

'Seems we've made landfall,' he told her, shipped the oars and swung over the side into the water. The boat did not list so dramatically this time, but:

'Adam!' she cried, tried to stand up but seemed rooted to the seat, her hands to the gunwales as he stood knee deep in the lake again. It felt much colder than before, because of the sweat he had raised from rowing the boat so fast.

'Stay put, Ruth,' he urged, waded along the side of the boat, took hold of the painter and tried to haul the craft up the beach clear of the water.

But the exertion of crossing the lake and the nervous tension that accompanied it had left him drained. He was unable to drag it for more than a foot or so after its bow became embedded in the shingle, and he told her in defeat:

'You'll have to get out here, Ruth.'

'Are you on dry land?'

'Yes.'

Something that sounded like a brief laugh of joy burst from her lips. Then she rose unsteadily to her feet, assured: 'Then there's no problem, Adam.'

She thought to pick up his rifle. And then it caused her no distress to get her shoes and the bottom of her dress wet as she climbed out of the boat he held from sliding back off the beach.

Then, before Steele was fully aware of what was happening, she half stumbled into him. He reached for the rifle he thought she was about to hand him. But heard it fall to the shingle, then felt her arms around him, her face pressing into his beard, her lips on his. And her body grinding against his, like she could not wait to express her feelings for him in the most fulsome and intimate way a woman can to a man.

Because she had taken him by surprise, there had been no time for him to draw breath and be ready. So he was forced to end the embrace and the kiss, pull himself away from her: suck in some damp morning air.

'Oh, thank you, thank you so much, Adam!' she gasped. 'I didn't get sick, did I? You didn't see me at my worst? But I must look absolutely dreadful now, and——'

She had to pause for breath now, and he was able to break in, said with what felt like a foolish grin:

'Thank you, Ruth. That was... But I have something to ask——'

'Here!' she said.

He was startled into silence not so much by the forceful way she spoke: instead by how she jerked aside her rainslicker, unfastened the top three buttons of her dress and then drove her hand inside like she was intent upon tearing it open.

'This is for you to take care of until it's needed.'

Buttons did not pop and she withdrew her hand without revealing anything more than her chest above the swells of her breasts: held it out toward him, her fist closed around a wad of bills.

'How did you ...?' he started.

She looked expectantly at him, waiting for him to finish.

He recognised that this time she had not been perceptive enough to read what he intended to ask. But then she shook her head to dismiss the query before he could finish it, went on unwittingly to answer it.

'As soon as I realised all that noise outside the hotel didn't mean anything good for us and we'd probably have to leave in a hurry, I decided the bag would only be a hindrance. So I just brought the money. Hid it where I thought it would be safest.'

'It'll still be safe there,' Steele told her, uncaring if she recognised how relieved he was.

She shook her head. 'No, Adam. Except for how we feel about each other, the money's all we have left.'

'I know, but——'

'And how you feel about me, Adam ... It has something to do with me being a woman, I hope?' she interrupted.

'It sure helps, Ruth,' he told her with the start of a grin.

She let him peer into her eager eyes for a stretched second. Then hung her head and turned it to the side, said quickly: 'At a time like this, money means nothing to me. It's much better I don't look after it.' She slowed the pace of what she was saying. 'I'm starting to regret I left my bag behind at that awful hotel. There's a lot of stuff in it a woman could use after what we've been through.' She sighed. 'My spectacles, too.'

'Ruth, I——'

'Take the money, Adam,' she insisted, stared into his bearded face, took his hand in hers and pressed the roll of bills into it. 'Now let's move on. I've shown you I trust you. If you take it and don't drop me along the way, then . . .'

He closed his hand around the money, pushed it into a pants pocket. Leaned forward, held her head gently in both hands and brushed his lips across her brow. Then he stooped to pick up his rifle from the beach, said: 'We don't even know which shore we're on, Ruth.'

He could have qualified this because he knew from the total silence all around—even the curlew had abandoned its mournful call—that the rowboat had not come about to land them back on the Broadwater side of the lake.

'You know something, Adam?' she asked, peering intently at him, unconcerned now that her appearance was far from its best.

'What?'

'North or south or east or west . . . I'm sure you'll know what's best for us to do.' She looked and sounded earnest.

He asked sardonically: 'You have some reason except for blind faith to think that, Ruth?'

He sloped the rifle to his shoulder as she reached for his free hand. And as they started up the beach side by side, she murmured:

'I just believe love can conquer all, Adam.'

He looked at her sharply.

She explained, a little nervously: 'Just before we got on that boat you said you hoped there would be the words. That's one neither of us have used before. Now I have and it's important to me you should believe I mean what I say?'

They came to a stop after the pressure of her hand in his

signalled it was what she wanted. He found himself compelled to peer into her earnestly expectant face.

'Well?' she asked anxiously.

'I don't know, Ruth.'

'Why not?'

'I'm not sure I know what it means.'

'You were married once. Albert told me so.'

'I don't think the two necessarily have to go——'

She nodded emphatically. 'Yes, you're right. But at least you know something that it doesn't mean? An awful lot of mistakes are made because——' She shrugged, showed a wan, sad smile. 'Let's hope this isn't another one, Adam?'

'We should learn by them, isn't that what they say? From what you told me about your marriage to Blair——'

She broke in grimly: 'Yes. I know I learned a lesson from that. Quite a few.'

'Do you reckon you know enough so you can teach me?' he asked with a grin. He released her hand to curl his arm around her waist, then let it fall until his fingers were splayed over the swell of her rear. 'Like I've never been taught before?'

She laughed, wriggled her rear wantonly under the pressure of his caress as they started across the beach again and murmured: 'So this is why they call you new students fresh men?'

11

They made slow and gentle love in the wet grass behind the shingle beach without taking off any articles of clothing. They were oblivious to where they were and its discomforts as they silently completed the act, so tenderly that in Steele's mind the memory of the first time in the bedroom at Trail's End was frenzied by comparison.

And yet it left them drained, incapable of positive movement or even thought for what seemed like a long time afterwards.

It was a good and unique experience for him and he guessed it was the same for her. And he wondered while they rested after the exhausting coupling if the uncertainty of the future had contributed to the near perfect matching of their emotions that had made it so magical at this time and in a place where so much was against them.

Then Ruth asked for a minute to herself and went back down the beach. Returned to ask: 'Do you know anything about this side of the lake, Adam?'

He saw she had washed her face in the lake, probably dried it as best she could on the already wet skirts of her dress. She had also fingercombed her hair into a semblance of order. But it was surely the glow of their love making shining in her eyes and shaping her mouth into a contented line that contributed as much as anything else to making her look more beautiful than he remembered. Maybe, too, his own deeper feeling for the woman helped, he allowed.

'A bunch of green hills and a lot of timber,' he told her as he sloped the rifle to his shoulder in the usual way. 'Which I've seen from the Broadwater side. I've been told there are some old gold mine workings left from the time when the town was no more than a couple of stores, a saloon and an assay office. And some farms. More of them derelict than are still worked.'

'Good country to get lost in?'

'If that's what we want,' he told her.

'Which we do, for as long as they're looking for us?'

'I reckon.'

She inserted her hand in his, intertwined their fingers, and invited: 'Lead on, partner. And who knows, we might stumble on some gold nuggets hidden by a crazy gold miner who forget where he left his cache?'

Steele had taken his fill of unreality. He was not about to indulge in fantasies. Now the wonder of their love making had faded, he was not in the mood to be anything less than practical about the rigors of the future.

But he was too grateful for the company of Ruth Blair to want to mar her moments of happiness.

The last thing he wanted from her, though, was chatter: especially foolish talk about the impossible coming true.

'Of course, I know there's absolutely no chance of that happening,' she said when her remark drew no response.

'Right,' he said, and stopped to listen to the silence now their footfalls had ceased to pad on the springy turf. He looked at her, saw she was frowning until she showed a brief smile, squeezed his hand to confirm she was not annoyed at him.

'If I start to prattle at the wrong time again, Adam, tell me to stop. This is all so totally new to me. I guess I just don't know how to act. What to do. Maybe I'm still deep down afraid. Like on the boat? But now I want to talk all the time, instead of not wanting to talk?'

'You're talking at the wrong time, Ruth,' he told her.

'Damn!'

He smiled briefly. 'But I can understand the reason.'

'Thanks. What are we listening for? When I'm not prattling on?'

'A creek.'

'A creek?'

He moved off again, staying close enough to the lake shore to see the beach on his left.

'In a fog like this, town streets can be easy. Especially if you know the town. I had to trust to luck crossing the lake, but at least I knew we'd keep going until we hit a shore. In this kind of country, the best way I know of making sure we don't go around in circles is to follow a creek. Back from where it reaches the lake.'

'Of course.' She made a sound of impatience with herself. 'And you think there's anything I can teach you?'

'You stick to giving lessons on the fun subjects, Ruth,' he told her lightly. 'And——'

He halted again, and held up the hand fisted around the rifle. She cocked her head to listen, then realised that this time he was looking rather than listening. She did the same, tilted her head to peer up at the pale white orb of the sun way off to their left, hanging above an invisible horizon.

'It's clearing.'

'Best we be away from the shore before it's all gone, Ruth. They're bound to figure it as one possibility that we crossed the lake. And if they spot us through a telescope they'll concentrate all their manpower over here.'

Aware the fog would probably lift quickly now the sun had started to burn it off, Steele abandoned his search for a stream. Began to lead Ruth by the hand away from the shore at a right angle. Hopeful the lake would remain shrouded in mist for as long as it took them to find more substantial cover for their escape.

From the start, they were climbing: moving up a steady grade through sodden, foot high ungrazed summer grass featured here and there with patches of rocky ground.

Ruth discovered the rocks first, and warned Steele to watch his step.

Then he was next to break the silence, after the grade had steepened enough to make them breathe hard and ooze sweat from their pores. After casting several glances over his shoulder, seen the pale sun brighten as the light all round changed from the grey to white, he said:

'It's thinning fast now, Ruth.'

'What?' she responded, the word little more than a grasp.

He did a double-take at her and realised that for a long time he had failed to see Ruth as more than just another feature of his surroundings. Now he recognised how weary she was as she struggled for breath and tried not to reveal this was what she was doing.

'Hey, you're almost out on your feet.'

'I'll be fine.' She sucked in a deep breath. 'Just as soon as we get to the top of this mountain and start down the other side.'

She showed him a grin that got some light into her eyes but could not shape her mouth into the appropriate line because of how she had to suck so much air into her lungs.

'It's far enough for awhile,' he said as he saw the dark shapes of some half buried rocks in the side of the hill a dozen feet away. They were of a height and shape that made them perfect to sit and rest on. He steered her to them, heard her grateful sigh as she sank down.

Then she said: 'I'm sorry for being such a . . . such a *woman*!'

'You did fine,' he assured her as he squatted on another rock, facing her. He grinned as he added: 'For the wife of a shoe store clerk. Who I reckon never climbed too far up a mountain before?'

She nodded and smiled wanly. 'They say Denver's a mile high from sea level. It's certainly in the mountains. But it's not a hilly city. And it has so many streetcars I was always surprised we sold as many pairs of shoes as we did.'

She looked around, exclaimed: 'My goodness, it's lifting really fast now, isn't it?'

They had gotten used to the weird sensation of isolation from being totally enclosed by fog that had reduced their visible world to a couple of square feet at worst, twice that at best. Now there was an even eerier quality about the way the fog had begun to disintegrate, thinning and retreating by the moment. Like the odourless smoke of a great fire, wafting away on all sides on a soft and silent breeze.

Within a minute of them sitting on the rocks the scene had altered dramatically, the sun suddenly blindingly bright so that everything above their elevated level was clear to see, sharp in outline. While below them was a smooth-surfaced sea of greyness that all the time was gradually sinking to bring more and more of the world into view in all directions.

Steele paid particular attention to the scene in the east: with the distant snow-capped ridges of the Sierra Nevadas, the closer foothills that dropped down in verdant steps toward the still-shrouded town and the lake on which it stood.

But only for a short while was he caught up in the sheer beauty of what he saw, unique to high country. Then he became aware of black streaks in the mist hiding the town across the lake, recognised it as chimney smoke.

'Best we get over the ridge,' he said as he stood up.

She looked to where he pointed with the rifle, about a hundred feet up to the crest of the hill they had been climbing blind, perhaps twice that in the distance they had to cover to reach it.

'Like I said at the start, Adam, lead on.'

She accepted his hand to help her to her feet. Then Steele tried not to hurry. But he was breathing as raggedly as Ruth from exertion and tension when they got to the hill crest.

A backward glance showed the roofs of the taller town buildings were sticking out through the smoke-stained mist. Ruth looked briefly at the same view and recognised they were in danger of being seen from Broadwater should anyone chance to gaze carefully across the lake from such a building toward this hilltop, one of the higher points on the western side of the lake.

And it was she who hurried forward to get over the brow of the hill first. But then she came to a sudden halt, raised an arm to point as she asked rhetorically: 'Will you look at that?'

There was less residual mist in the hollows and valleys spread to this western side of the hill and the scene below where Steele came to a stop beside the woman was clear to see. And there in the bottom land of a short north to south valley was a small farmstead comprised of a group of three buildings and some cultivated fields bounded by fences, surrounded by open pasture.

'Doesn't it look marvellous, Adam?'

'It sure does, Ruth,' he replied as he raked an unblinking gaze over the spread.

'And you know what looks best of all to me right now?'

'What's that?' he answered as they started down the hillside in unison without holding hands or any other kind of physical contact now.

'The smoke rising from the chimney,' she told him and a spontaneous laugh escaped her throat as a measure of the joy she experienced after enduring so much tension for so long.

'Let's hope there's a good country breakfast cooking on the stove, Ruth.' He was still concentrating his attention on the farm. 'Seems like a long time since we never got to eat the supper you cooked last evening.'

'Well . . . That, too,' she allowed. 'But first of all I'd like some hot water and soap to make a start at feeling human again.'

'You know something?' he asked, allowing himself to be caught up in her infectious brand of happiness now his survey of the well cared for place in the valley had revealed nothing of which to be suspicious.

'Tell me.'

'I think I like you best when you're an animal!'

She hit him playfully on the upper arm and laughed more freely than before as they had to prevent themselves from hurrying on the downslope toward the farm.

The closer they got to the property, that was spread over some twenty acres of fenced off land, the more Steele found he had to work at matching his mood to that of Ruth. For it was difficult not to draw comparisons between this place and the one he had been forced to leave. And to brood on the fact that Trail's End was surely gone forever as far as he was concerned.

The farmstead reminded him of Trail's End only in terms of the loving care that had so obviously been lavished upon it. In all other respects, the two places were totally different.

Here there was a two-story house, stone below and timber above under a peaked tile roof. Which stood behind a yard of mown grass bounded on the three open sides by flower-filled borders. Irregular-shaped flagstones were set into the lawn, a pace apart, between the unporched front door and the wagon-wide track that came in from the north and ended at the farm. Out back was another yard enclosed by a stable on one side, a barn facing this and a plot filled with healthy looking vegetables across from the house.

Wheat, cotton and fodder crops grew in the larger fields and there was an orchard of fruit trees at one side of the house. Water was available from a natural pond out back of the orchard.

The frames of the gleaming house windows had been newly white painted so recently that the smell of paint was discernible in the air, along with woodsmoke infiltrated with the mouthwatering aroma of frying bacon.

'Do you know something, Adam?' Ruth asked happily as

they reached the bottom of the slope and started along the wheel-rutted and hoof-pocked track that curled around the front of the house and ended behind the barn.

'Tell me,' he echoed her response of a few moments ago as he had to work harder than ever at seeming light hearted while he recalled bright summer mornings at Trail's End, when woodsmoke mixed with cooking fragrances made a man so glad to be alive at the start of a fine new day.

His actual mood was also influenced by the way he instinctively looked for fresh sign on the track. And tried to see beyond the neat, peaceful façade of the farm to sense lurking danger: or, at least, an indication they would not receive a friendly welcome here.

'I'll be willing to stay dirty while I eat,' Ruth said as she took the lead in crossing th. 'awn on the flagstone pathway, a smile on her face and a spring in her step.

She was clearly not troubled by any doubts of her own about her idyllic surroundings: unconcerned that the people who lived on such an isolated place, lavishing every spare moment on it, might be less than well disposed toward the two strangers about to disturb them this early morning that had changed so rapidly from foggy to bright sunlight.

A bearded man with a rifle sloped to his shoulder and eyes that were filled with a strange mixture of regret and suspicion. And a foolishly smiling woman who was giving the impression she did not have a care in the world.

Both of them bedraggled looking in rain slickers over water- and mud-stained, crumpled and creased clothing. Who, close up, probably smelled bad to anyone except each other. Especially anyone who lived in such a spick and span place as this.

'Ruth, I think we——' Steele started.

She looked over her shoulder at him, then quickly to the front again as he broke off. This as the door latch was lifted and the door swung inward and a woman of fifty or so appeared on the threshold.

A short, thickly built woman dressed in a white blouse and black skirt with a pink apron tied around her waist. She had brown hair turning grey that was held in a bun on top of her head, and a round, healthily brown face that in respose

113

probably showed few wrinkles. But she was smiling brightly toward her visitors and deep lines were cut in the flesh at each side of her pleasure-filled eyes and her full lips, drawn back to display white, perfectly shaped teeth.

Both her hands were plunged deep into the voluminous front pocket of her apron.

'Heavens, whatever have you to been up to?' she greeted cheerfully, like she was mildly rebuking a pair of mischievous children. 'Just look at you? Why, it appears you might have walked across this entire country. And hardly rested for a minute while you were doing it.'

The food frying in a skillet on the stove provided the strongest and most appealing aroma to emerge from the open doorway. But it was also possible to catch the smell of polish and of soap: this latter on the flesh of the woman, maybe her recently laundered clothing.

'Not quite that far, ma'am,' Steele said as he tipped his hat with his free hand.

'Oh, I just knew there would be friendly people living in such a fine looking home as this, Mrs . . .' Ruth said enthusiastically.

'Cramer, young lady,' the brightly smiling woman supplied. 'Me and Thomas, my husband, we're well known for making folks feel welcome. Even though, living way out here the way we do, we don't get too many callers.'

'Goodness you don't know how much this means to us,' Ruth said. And once more revealed how her priorities had changed when she could not stop herself from breathing in deeply through her nose, relishing the cooking fragrances that dominated the atmosphere of the room.

'Yes, a real warm welcome is what we aim to extend to strangers,' Mrs Cramer said. Then she raised her voice to call: 'Isn't that right, Thomas?'

At precisely the moment when she readied herself for the shout, and the smile began to fade, Steele realised his instinct for lurking danger had failed to warn him something was wrong here. But he did not waste valuable thinking time with futile self anger as he heard a man order coldly:

'Drop that rifle, mister. Or you and the woman get a barrel each.'

Ruth snapped her head around and Steele moved with less

114

haste to look to the left: toward the front corner of the house that had been on their blind side ever since they came down off the slope and started along the track.

They saw Thomas was of similar age and stature to his wife and that he was attired in denim work clothes that were as clean and fresh as hers. It was not possible to see much of his face beneath his bright sandy-coloured hair because he was aiming a double barrel shotgun across the front of the house: levelled from the shoulder, his face pressed to the stock and largely obscured by his hands.

'Thomas has never been known to say anything he didn't mean, you folks,' Mrs Cramer warned. 'But I do lie sometimes, when the occasion calls for it.'

As Ruth gasped, Steele kept his head turned toward Thomas Cramer but shifted his eyes along their sockets to look at the woman who had earlier created such a false strong impression of downhome friendliness.

Now she eyed her visitors with unconcealed contempt as she drew one hand out of her apron pocket and levelled a revolver at Ruth's belly, clicked back the hammer.

Despite the heavy menace of the situation, Steele found himself registering that the Purdy shotgun aimed by Cramer and the Remington levelled by his wife looked as well tended as everything else about the place.

'Adam!' Ruth rasped, and stepped back alongside him, to hook a hand over his forearm and dig in her fingers.

'We don't ever make strangers welcome,' Mrs Cramer said. 'On account of we never get strangers calling on us. As a rule. Especially we don't get killers stopping by to——'

'Mathilde!' her husband cut in grimly.

'Thomas?'

'Quit your gabbing, woman. Just be sure to keep them covered with the pistol.'

He began to advance across the front of the house, stepped over the start of the flower border and on to the lawn. Inevitably, the shotgun was not trained at his targets with such a rock steady aim now he was moving.

Steele remained perturbed for just a moment by how the Cramers knew he was wanted for murder. This as he struggled to rid his mind of an image of two blood-run corpses sprawled on the ground in this appealing place under the bright, summer morning sky.

Ruth and himself. Or Thomas and Mathilde Cramer? Or not dead, maybe. The flesh torn and bleeding, bones smashed and organs mutilated, but the mind still active and able to demand full-throated screams because of the searing pain from awesome injuries.

Steele alone deserved to suffer that kind of punishment. Or to die. For was he not wanted, as Al Strachen had said, dead or alive?

Not the neat-looking, fresh-smelling woman who held a revolver. Nor her equally well turned out husband with the double barrel shotgun. Certainly not the hapless, worried by her unkept appearance Ruth Blair.

But he had to make the decision and act upon it, in full knowledge of the risk he was taking with the lives of three innocent people. And there was no opportunity in these circumstances to warn any of them about the kind of mortal danger they were going to be in as he said thickly:

'I know the feeling, Mr Cramer. Isn't that so, Ruth?'

'What?'

'What?'

Ruth and Cramer voiced the query in perfect unison. The woman was afraid, the man irritated.

Steele's face remained impassively set above the beard as he continued to keep the element of surprise on his side when he said evenly: 'How some women talk too much when they——'

Cramer snarled across what the Virginian was saying: 'I told you to drop that rifle, mister!'

Steele nodded and began to ease the Colt Hartford slowly down from his shoulder without altering his apparently relaxed stance and his expression. Like he intended to comply with the instruction. But a moment later he abruptly moved fast. Tore his free arm out of Ruth's grasp and swung behind her. Gave her a powerful shove in the back with his shoulder. So she was sent staggering forward into the doorway, across the threshold and crashed into the Cramer woman.

He heard both of them vent shrill cries of alarm and pain. Ignored them to look toward Cramer as he lunged in the wake of Ruth and took a double-handed grip on the Colt Hartford, forefinger curled around the trigger as he thumbed back the hammer.

The short and broadly built farmer was still shocked by the sudden flurry of violent action. Which delayed his response to it. And when he did act he panicked and squeezed both triggers at once.

Steele was in the cover of the doorway by then, fully turned around, just the muzzle of the rifle out in the open.

The twin reports of the discharging shotgun briefly blanketed the shrieks and curses of the woman who were now evidently engaged in a struggle that went beyond hurling abuse at each other. But Steele could not spare the time to see what was happening in the house as buckshot sprayed across the open doorway to harmlessly pepper the wall, the lawn and the far flower border.

At least there had been no shot from within the house, which maybe augered well for the outcome of what was happening in there.

As Steele leaned forward to look toward the farmer, he saw Cramer continued to be the main danger. The man was doing some less loud but more obscene cursing of his own: his anger for the moment directed at the inanimate Purdy which he had broken open and now was struggling to extract the expended shellcases from the reeking breeches.

'How'd you find out about me, feller?' Steele asked as he stepped outside, having seen Cramer could do nothing until he had reloaded. He even had time to glance beyond the farmer and over his own shoulder toward the other front corner of the house.

But the Cramers had made their play without help. Just the lowing of a cow, the clucking of some hens and the snorting of horses troubled by the gunfire provided signs of life elsewhere on the farmstead.

Then he took a moment to look back through the doorway. Saw an immaculately clean, elegantly furnished parlour. Once neat and tidy, the room was now in process of being violently disarrayed as the two women struggled for possession of the Remington.

Both had a hand upon it at full arm's reach above their heads. Swayed from side to side as they continued to trade

117

curses: close enough for the saliva of each snarled word to spray into the other's face.

'The frigging law, who else?' Cramer growled at Steele and intensified his efforts to reload the broken open shotgun as the shrieking of the women told him his wife was locked in a struggle he could not see.

'How'd they know we came across the lake?' Steele asked.

Cramer drew out the old cases with a shaking hand, tossed them down and reached into a bulging pocket of his dungarees for a pair of new cartridges.

'No cold-blooded killer ever outsmarts Gavin Fenton, mister!' One of the cartridges sprang out of his shaking hand. 'He made sure all the ways to escape were covered.'

'Now it's your turn to throw down the gun, feller,' Steele instructed, with the passing thought that he should have counted on the Broadwater sheriff despatching deputies around the lake.'

'Up your ass, killer!' Cramer countered, too deep in a turmoil of anger and panic and maybe terror to recognise he had no chance of winning this confrontation as Steele advanced on him, Colt Hartford levelled from the hip.

The Virginian had no intention of shooting down the farmer: had just a single-handed grip on the rifle when he reached Cramer, pushed out his other hand to grasp the twin barrels of the broken open shotgun and wrenched the weapon out of the man's trembling grip.

He saw Cramer had once been a handsome man. But fire had badly burned the left side of his face, left the flesh shrivelled and puckered, dried and drained of moisture. His left eye had been burned out in the fire, which was maybe why the other one was filled with such a high degree of blazing hatred as he shifted its stare from the shotgun snatched out of his hand, to the single shell in his other hand, then at Steele's face.

The Virginian dropped the shotgun and tensed, ready to meet an attack. But then the handgun exploded in the house and during the moment of silence that came in its wake it was like the crack had been louder and more dramatic than the report of the two barrels of the shotgun.

'Matty!' Cramer roared, and lunged forward.

He swerved past the Virginian who whirled around, just as

anxious as the other man to find out what had happened inside the house. And Steele was just a part second behind the distraught farmer in plunging through the doorway. Where both came to abrupt halts and surveyed the scene.

Cramer uttered a low, strangled moan and seemed rooted to the spot as he stared at where his wife was sprawled on her back on the floor, one side of her face run with blood which still oozed from a hole in her temple. Some had splashed down over her blouse when she was shot and looked a more vivid shade of crimson against the white fabric than on her weather burnished skin.

'My God, I've killed a person!' Ruth blurted, her voice high pitched and weak.

She turned just her head to look at the two men standing near the doorway. Her hands hung down at her sides and there was a soft clunk as the Remington, smoke still wisping from the muzzle, dropped from her shock-loosened grasp and fell to a rug.

Cramer sprang suddenly out of his state of suspended animation: needed to voice his feelings before he acted on them, yelled! 'You murderin' bitch!'

He lunged forward and started to stoop toward the discarded revolver.

Ruth watched him, no flicker of fear visible on her face that continued to express depthless remorse.

And Cramer recognised that in her state of mind the woman was powerless to defend herself and he changed his plan. Ignored the gun on the floor, straightened up and went for the woman: his hands clawed ready to fasten around her throat.

She made no move to back away from him.

Steele's first instinct was to blast a bullet into the broad back of the grief maddened man. But he checked the impulse. Not from any feeling for the man. Instead because he was worried that at such a short range the Colt Hartford would blast the bullet completely through his body into Ruth.

He hurled aside the shotgun. Swung the Colt Hartford high and brought it down hard, to smash the barrel across the centre of Cramer's head.

The man's outstretched hands were only inches from Ruth's vulnerable throat when the blow struck and he was abruptly unconscious on his feet. Fell forward with his arms still reaching out in front of him, unwittingly took her shoulders in a limp embrace.

And still Ruth was unwilling or incapable of backing off from him. But she had the strength to remain ramrod stiff as the man's forward momentum banged him against her. Then he slid down her in a series of near erotic moves: dropped to his knees in front of her so his face trailed between her breasts, his arms and then hands dragged over them and he nuzzled her crotch before he tipped to the side, collapsed into an untidy heap on the floor at her feet.

Blood oozed from a wound in his head, clashed with the sandy hue of his hair. But he began to breathe deeply and regularly and so obviously was not going to die.

Whereas there was that brand of inertia about his wife's form that signalled she would never breathe again. And this awesomeness of new death acted to focus the attention of Steele and Ruth on her.

Steele's eyes were impassive, the woman's vacant. He looking upon violent death for the latest of many occasions, she probably driven into a state of deep shock by witnessing it for the first time. Certainly she had never been responsible for it before.

She was still in the grip of the trauma when Steele stepped around the unconscious Thomas Cramer and squatted beside the corpse of the man's wife. Made physically certain of what he was talking about before he said:

'She's dead, Ruth. And I know it was an accident.'

It was like she had heard only the sound of the Virginian's voice, not what he had told her. There was a mechanical tone in her voice when she said: 'It was an accident. I never meant to kill her. We both held the gun. It just went off. It could have been me who ...'

Steele rose to his feet as Ruth's voice trailed away. She continued to look at the corpse while his mind raced out of control for stretched seconds. His thoughts concerned with how there was a whole area open for discussion about the two of them knowing how it was an accident. Or three, if Thomas Cramer could be persuaded to provide a truthful account of what happened.

But none of that would be to any avail. For Ruth was in the indefensible position of being an accessory after the fact of the long-ago murder of Jim Bishop. And she had willingly taken flight with Steele. Therefore it would be impossible to convince any court that she had accidentally shot somebody who was endeavouring to apprehend the fugitives.

Steele shook his head, to try to physically dislodge this time-wasting line of thought from his mind. But he immediately felt sick to his stomach as he was forced to face a just as awesome truth. That he had initiated the series of events which had culminated in this tragedy.

And what if the Remington had gone off in Mathilde Cramer's hand at the moment he had impelled Ruth toward her?

'Ruth,' Steele said thickly as he hooked an arm around her shoulder. 'You have to know that——'

She nodded and vented a soft cry of despair as the rigidity went out of her and she leaned against him, trembled from head to toe as she broke in: 'You did what you thought was right, Adam. Better them than us, uh?'

She peered up into his face and looked like a child seeking reassurance.

'That sure is right,' he told her. 'But I was going to——'

'To tell me that if we get caught, I won't have a snowball's chance in hell of being believed?'

'I'm afraid that's right, also,' he told the frowning woman.

She shivered more violently, said with intense feeling gleaming in her eyes that looked larger than he had seen them before: 'Do me a favour, Adam?'

'Whatever you want.'

'Don't talk about being afraid. I'm certain I'm scared enough for the both of us.'

'Easy, Ruth.' He held her more tightly and fought against a compulsion to unburden himself to her of his guilt for what had happened, all of which it was impossible not to regard as his fault.

But he had enough self control to recognise this was not the place and they probably did not have the time to indulge in that kind of exchange. It helped when he saw her wan smile, seemingly of understanding, before she told him:

121

'And I'll try not to be such a ... Oh, such a *woman*!' She sagged more heavily against him and it took him momentarily off guard. So he almost did not take a more secure hold on her in time to prevent her sliding to the floor between the unconscious Cramer and his dead wife. She had passed out cold.

'Sure, Ruth,' he growled, let go of the Colt Hartford and picked her up in both arms. 'Women faint, but men aren't allowed to be faint-hearted.'

12

Steele turned one way then the other, searching for a place to put down the limp weight of the unconscious woman. He saw a comfortable-looking sofa but ignored it. Only fleetingly considered taking her through an open doorway beyond which he could see the foot of a stairway that presumably led up to the bedrooms.

He did not think Ruth would appreciate the comfort he sought for her if it entailed waking up in the home of the woman she had killed. So he continued to cradle her in his arms as he completed his shuffling turns, found himself facing the open front door and went toward it.

He had to step sideways over the threshold to keep from banging Ruth's head and legs against the doorframe. Then heard a sharp intake of breath and froze, tensed to feel a bullet drill into his back. The aroma of cooking food, which he had not been aware of for a long time, abruptly filled his nostrils from within the house. A familiar voice instructed:

'Stay that way, Steele!' A second went by, then Al Strachen cleared his throat and repeated the point he had made last night. 'You're under arrest for the murder of deputy James Bishop. The warrant states dead or alive. Nothing has changed.'

Steele did not strictly obey the order. He turned his head to look across the front of the house at the six-feet tall, leanly-built man with the hangdog look. This morning Strachen was dressed the same as last night, except he now wore a grey Stetson instead of the black derby. He was unshaven and looked bone-deep weary. But Steele thought he detected a trace of elation, maybe tinged with regret, visible in the man's eyes. He was sure the regret was not on account of him or the passing of the good-working relationship they had shared during the weeks at Trail's End.

'Wrong, something has changed,' Strachen went on. His tone had hardened as he pushed the Colt further out in front of him, aimed at Steele's head as he moved to close with his target, careful to step around the discarded, broken-open Purdy on the lawn. 'I don't prefer it should be alive anymore. Be a pleasure to kill you, Steele.'

'But you won't, Marshal. Unless he does something to make it so you have no alternative.'

This was another familiar voice. And Steele halted the turn toward Strachen, to look at the other corner of the house. Where the six-feet tall, two hundred pounds in weight, broad-shouldered, narrow-waisted and long-legged Sheriff Gavin Fenton had stepped into sight. His face was as gentle looking as it always was in repose and he looked totally at ease with his right hand draped over the jutting butt of his holstered Colt while he held an unlit pipe in his other hand.

He was flanked by two deputies. On one side the thirty-years-old, good looking, tall and broad Luke Dexter and on the other a thickly-moustached man of the same age who was faintly familiar to Steele. His left hand was heavily bandaged and the Virginian thought he was the one who had cut himself on the broken window at the Tivoli.

The two deputies had Winchester rifles sloped to their shoulders. All three Broadwater lawmen wore badges which gleamed in the morning sunlight.

'Is Ruth badly hurt?' Strachen asked before Steele could say anything to Fenton and the deputies.

'She fainted, that's all,' Steele replied and put his back to the open doorway so he could see all four lawmen by just moving his head from one side to the other. 'How did you fellers know we came——'

'When your luck turns bad, it really does go sour on you, Steele,' Fenton cut in. 'I sent a man around the lake soon as we knew it was you and your ladyfriend skipped out of that rathole of a hotel Clyde Barlow runs. To warn folks on this side of the water.'

'The Cramers were warned,' Steele growled.

'But Ray Paxton here,' Fenton went on, gestured with his

124

pipe to the deputy with the bandaged hand, 'he figured it would be quicker for a man to row across the lake than ride around it. This was a little later, after we knew you'd got away under cover of the fog. But what I mean about your luck being so bad, that boat you stole belonged to Ray Paxton.'

The deputy scowled at Steele.

Fenton continued: 'Soon as we knew about the boat being gone, well . . .' He shrugged his broad shoulders. 'We mounted up and we all of us rode around the lake. Split into four-man groups to check all the places and——'

'When we heard the shooting from the Cramer place——' Luke Dexter tried to take up the account of the search.

But Fenton interrupted him: 'Did anybody get hurt bad? Tom and Matty Cramer?'

He was suddenly worried, and tried to peer in through the nearest polished window in the newly-painted frame. But lace curtaining obscured his view.

'He'll get up, she won't,' Steele said, his arms starting to ache with the weight of Ruth.

'Shit!' Fenton snarled, and replaced the pipe in the shirt pocket to which his badge was pinned. He slid his Colt out of the holster and aimed it at Steele. 'They were a fine couple. Ran a fine place. Decent, good people. Lower that woman slow and easy, Steele. And don't make any move for the doorway. Or for that knife you keep in your boot.'

'I'm glad to have your full co-operation at last, Sheriff,' Strachen said with undisguised sarcasm.

Steele was deeply concerned with his predicament. Sure that in a lifetime of being in tight spots, this was the toughest of all. He spared no more than a passing thought to the implication that until now Fenton had been less than enthusiastic about helping the United States marshal apprehend a man with whom he had a degree of rapport: maybe even a sneaking brand of admiration. Just as he admired all good and decent, hardworking people who were in the minority in the wide open town where he was peace officer.

But the situation that had existed before was totally immaterial as Dexter and Paxton took their cues from Fenton and swung their rifles down to aim them from the hip at Steele.

'It was an——' Ruth started to say, speaking as if in her

sleep, rolling her head on Steele's arm like she was on the point of waking up.

'What's she saying?' Strachen demanded and advanced on Steele, thrusting his revolver in the holster tied down to his right thigh. 'Here, give her to me. Keep him covered, you men.'

'Damn right!' Fenton snapped as he closed with the Virginian from the other side. 'Pass her over to her brother, Steele. And move away from the door!'

Steele thought grimly that it was certainly right that he had never been backed into a tighter corner than this. And for a tense, stretched second he had never felt more suicidal in terms of attempting to escape against odds stacked so high against him he knew he could not possibly survive.

But having this woman in his arms, on the brink of coming out of helpless unconsciousness, acted to check the impulse to throw away his life. As he had risked throwing it away when he made his move against the Cramers. Put her life on the line, too.

But that had been a different situation. The hapless farmer and his wife were good and decent people. Not used to holding guns on their fellow man. Capable of making blustering threats, but inevitably reluctant to carry them out. The kind of people who would also take a vital moment to consider the consequences before they committed the act of squeezing a trigger.

But he was faced by four men who were professional users of firearms. Had experienced the consequences of using them: knew they could well end up dead if they wasted the shortest span of time before they committed the act.

But it was not because of the greater danger to Ruth that he held back from making any reckless move. For a moment after he transferred the woman to the scowling Strachen who quickly backed off to take her out of the line of fire from the Broadwater lawman, he still felt the same.

Because, despite losing everything else that had made his life worth living until . . . God, only a little more than twelve hours ago, he now had the love of this woman who exerted so much influence on him she was worth more than all that other stuff put together. And as long as she continued to love him, he was willing to fight for his freedom if there was a damn good chance of survival.

'It was an accident,' Ruth insisted, still in the twilight world between insensibility and wakefulness. 'I never meant to kill her. The gun just went off and...'

'Shush, Ruth, it's all right now,' her brother soothed as he backed off and squatted on his haunches, set her down on the still damp grass.

'Strachen's sister killed Matty Cramer?' Fenton asked, coming to an abrupt halt as he was about to swing in through the doorway of the house.

'Like she's saying, it was an accident,' Steele said.

He raised his hands to shoulder height in response to how Paxton gestured with his rifle.

'Shit,' Fenton rasped. It was the second obscenity spoken in a short time by a man who seldom used bad language.

Steele said as the Broadwater man went into the house: 'I cracked Cramer over the head. And I'm also responsible for his wife being shot.'

'You don't have to protect Ruth!' Strachen snapped, rising to his feet and drawing his Colt to again aim it at Steele. 'The law's the law, without any exceptions. She's already wanted for hindering a US marshal in the execution of his duty. You men keep him well covered.'

'You bet,' Paxton said and Steele was again aware this deputy eyed him with greater dislike than any of the other lawmen. Wondered in passing if this was because he had stolen the man's boat. Or maybe Paxton blamed him for breaking the window on which he injured his hand.

'We may be hick town deputies, but we know how to secure a prisoner,' Dexter growled in a way that indicated the Broadwater men were not well disposed toward the federal marshal. Were now able to feel superior to him since it was Strachen who had let a prisoner escape when he should have been secure at Trail's End.

'Albert!' Ruth exclaimed, and struggled up into a sitting position on the lawn.

Strachen looked down at her. 'Are you all right, Ruth?'

Fenton called from inside the house, his voice grim: 'One dead and one out cold, just like Steele said.'

'Whatever else Adam said, I killed that poor woman,' Ruth

muttered, and rose unsteadily to her feet.

'Stay there for a while, Ruth,' Strachen urged her. 'We'll get all the details later.'

'But I insist——' Ruth started to protest.

Strachen whirled on her, thrust his gun forward, the expression of blazing-eyed fury contorting his face warning he was close to blasting a bullet into his suddenly terrified sister.

At that moment, when every stunned gaze was fixed on Strachen, Steele might in different circumstances have attempted to break free of this tight corner: to hell with the consequences. But the only movement he made was the flick of his eyes across their narrowed sockets. For he was certain Strachen would not squeeze the trigger to kill his sister. Not right there and then.

Then the enraged marshal regained firm control of himself, spoke in an ice-cold tone. 'You're in no position to insist on anything, Ruth. Steele is under arrest for murder, you for aiding and abetting his flight from justice. If either of you try to escape again, be warned. I'll be within my rights, and I won't hesitate to use whatever means are necessary to prevent it. Which includes killing you. Sister or not!'

It was several seconds before Ruth could tear her gaze free of her brother's stare. Then she looked fearfully around, unable to focus on anything or anybody for a long time. Finally she located Steele and looked at him with total helplessly as she said: 'He means it, Adam.'

Steele nodded. 'I know it, Ruth,' he said, and meant that. He had decided that the US marshal seldom lost his temper and never totally lost his grip on self control. But in cold blood, to uphold the law he was capable of just about anything.

Now Strachen cleared his throat, let the pent up breathe whistle softly out between pursed lips. Then drew them back in a quiet smile of satisfaction as he said: 'You better believe it, Steele. I've got you good and for all this time.'

Ruth took a single staggering step on unsteady legs, reached for and found the front wall of the house to keep herself from going down on the lawn again.

Paxton said to Dexter: 'Guess somebody should go bring the horses.'

'And round up the rest of the boys from all over,' Dexter said.

Gavin Fenton stepped from the doorway of the house, his revolver holstered so he had both hands free to tamp tobacco into the bowl of his pipe as he advised: 'I figure you got no alternative but to come quietly, Steele.'

'What I intend to do, Sheriff,' the Virginian replied wearily and showed a faint smile that drew no matching response from the pale looking Ruth as he added: 'It's been quite a night for both of us. I reckon what we're sorely in need of is a rest.'

13

Ray Paxton went to bring the four horses from where they were left when the twin discharge of the shotgun signalled that the fugitives were probably at the Cramer house.

Then both the deputies rode away from the farmstead to round up the other members of the posse that had raced around the lake, split into small groups to try to pick up sign of Steele and Ruth.

Strachen had a set of heavy iron manacles in a saddlebag and wasted no time in padlocking the bracelets to Steele's wrists. After they were in place, some two feet of thick linked chain allowed the prisoner a degree of freedom as he sat in the parlour of the Cramer house, which the pipe-smoking Fenton had fixed up a little by draping the corpse with a blanket and straightening furniture which had been overturned during the death struggle.

Steele sat in a comfortable easy chair, Strachen close by in a hard-seated, straight-backed chair with the covered body of Mathilde Cramer at his feet.

Thomas Cramer, still unconscious, had been lifted on to the sofa and Gavin Fenton attended to cleaning and dressing his wound while Ruth was in the kitchen, finishing off the breakfast the dead woman had started to cook.

It was Ruth who suggested she finish making breakfast and was given disinterested permission by her brother.

No one expressed any enthusiasm for eating at first, but as the smells of food and coffee got stronger, it seemed to Steele the other men's appetites were being whetted as much as his own.

Ruth herself could not face the food after she served the breakfast of ham, eggs, grits and coffee to Steele, Strachen and Fenton: and she volunteered to take over the chore of watching for Thomas Cramer to regain consciousness.

The men ate off plates balanced on their laps. This was at the insistence of Gavin Fenton who considered it would not be right to mess up the place worse than it was already. During a cursory exploration of the house to see that everything was secure enough to leave for awhile, he had seen that in the kitchen, as neat and sparkling clean as everywhere else, the table was ready set for two.

'They were just about to sit down and have breakfast like always when you two showed up,' the Broadwater sheriff said to end a long silence disturbed only by eating sounds.

'They were the first to point guns at us!' Ruth countered.

'Shush,' her brother said.

'Rather listen to talk than chomping and scraping,' Fenton said. He gestured with his fork. 'Must be having that poor woman laying dead there on the floor.'

'We just came here for——' Ruth started and suddenly stopped.

Everyone looked toward the sofa, thinking she interrupted what she was saying because there had been a sudden change in the condition of the unconscious man. But they saw Ruth was looking pensively into space. Then she peered at Steele, asked:

'What did we come here for, Adam?'

Steele stopped eating breakfast under the restraints of the manacles that seemed to get more heavy by the moment, answered evenly: 'Get something to eat and a couple of horses if they had them to spare. I was going to pay for the food and the animals.'

'I bet,' Strachen interjected.

'Steele's known for always paying his way,' Fenton put in.

'With your sister's money,' the Virginian told Strachen morosely.

The marshal snarled at Ruth: 'You gave him your money as well as your body?'

'Hey now!' Fenton snapped, working on his image of being something of a prude despite having to maintain law and order in such a wide-open town as Broadwater. 'In this house, with a woman newly dead, I'll be obliged if you'll watch your tongue, Marshal!'

He glared at Strachen and the federal man looked ready to

take issue with the local sheriff. Then he shrugged, said with a faint sneer: 'Ruth's a widow woman long past her age of innocence. So what she does and who she chooses to do it with is up to her.'

'Precisely, Albert,' Ruth countered. 'And after being married to Eversly Blair for so long, seeing him go out and kick over the traces while I stayed faithfully at home minding the store, I think I deserve some kind of better life.'

'I warned you not to marry Blair,' he reminded her.

'I know you did. I'm not blaming you for that.'

'I just wish I was there to warn you about Steele before you and he . . .' He glanced at Fenton, changed what he intended to say and finished lamely: 'But even if I did, I don't suppose it would have made any difference to you: the kind of strong-willed woman you've become? You'd still have thrown in your lot with him.'

Thomas Cramer groaned like he would soon wake up. Ruth looked at him, then at Steele, the blanket-draped corpse, paid scant attention to Fenton and finally gazed bleakly at her brother to ask:

'What's the use, Albert? I just hope one day you meet someone and won't right away start looking for their faults. Someone who'll make such an impression on you it won't matter what she is or what she's done. Maybe then you'll start to act like a human being. Enough to see that nobody's as perfect as you think you are and——'

She broke off as Cramer made a series of more obtrusive sounds.

Fenton gulped down a final mouthful of his breakfast, put his empty plate aside to go to the sofa, said: 'You people best save your family squabbles until a different time. And you, Mrs Blair, better not be within reach of Tom Cramer when he comes to. Or maybe he'll do something he'll regret later.'

She nodded miserably, rose wearily from where she was sitting beside the unconscious man, moved to sit on the arm of the chair where Steele sat.

'No, Ruth!' Strachen ordered sharply. He moderated his tone but his expression remained hard as he explained to his startled sister: 'I don't want you and your . . . your friend too close. That way, you can't connive to do anything like you did at his ranch.'

He gingerly touched the top of his head, recalling rather than experiencing the pain of the crack with the shovel handle.

'We did not connive, and you well know it, Albert! It was entirely my own idea——'

'I said no family squabbles here, you people!' Fenton growled.

He bent over Cramer who had recovered enough to be stringing sentences together in a way that made sense. Revealed he could recall the violence of his wife's death and the two people who had brought tragedy into his life this morning. Then he vented some disjointed obscenities, began to thrash his hands about.

Fenton shifted so his body obscured Cramer's view of the room, and reached down to restrain the grief-stricken, vengeance-bent man. Turned his head to snarl: 'Get them out of here, Strachen! Put them in the barn or the stable or someplace until we're ready to leave!'

Strachen looked about to protest, resentful of being given orders by the Broadwater lawman. But then he caught a glimpse of the suddenly dumbstruck rage of Cramer's fire-scarred face and rose fast, forgot about his plate and tipped the remains of his breakfast on the floor in his hurry to do as Fenton asked.

Cramer began to shriek more loudly and obscenely.

Strachen snatched the gun from his holster, waved it carelessly between Steele and his sister as he ordered: 'All right! On your feet, mister! Get out of here! Move it! You, too, Ruth! For your own good!'

Steele rose smoothly to his feet, holding his plate in one manacled hand. Ruth came to get it. By tacit agreement, both refused to be provoked to haste by Strachen's attitude and Ruth set the plate down on a table then allowed herself to be ushered out of the house by Steele. He thought she derived as much satisfaction as he did from staying calm in the ambience of high tension generated by others in the room.

It was a childish sensation to relish, he acknowledged as they moved out on to the lawn where the mid-morning sun felt uncomfortably hot, but they were helpless prisoners and had to get what they could from the situation.

Strachen growled resentfully: 'That country town lawman sure does have an inflated opinion of his own importance.'

'He's a big fish in a small pool around here,' Steele said, glad he still had his hat on since there was no shade in the front yard of the Cramer house.

'He's a pain in the ass, that's what he is!' Strachen snarled and pushed the revolver back in his holster.

As Ruth curled a hand around one of his arms, Steele allowed: 'People who are good at what they do can be that sometimes.'

'You think I'm not?' Strachen shifted his angry gaze away from the doorway to direct it at Steele.

'You're a good man to have around a ranch when there's work to be done, feller.'

'I know,' the US marshal said, his anger abating as galloping hoofbeats sounded in the distance, the riders coming down the track from the north, still out of sight beyond the hill over which Steele and Ruth had come from the lake shore. 'I do what I have to do in my line of work. And tracking you from the east after all those years, that wasn't a bad job, I figure?'

'If I was paying you, I wouldn't have any cause for complaint,' Steele said.

Strachen pursed his lips, gave an almost imperceptible shake of his head before he allowed: 'As a ranch boss, you're a good man to work for, Steele.'

'But that doesn't matter to you at all, does it?' Ruth demanded scornfully of her brother as Cramer again began to yell and curse inside the house, until the beating of hooves of the approaching horses masked his shrieking voice.

Strachen shook his head emphatically, said grimly: 'Like us being brother and sister, Ruth.' Then he had to shout louder by the moment to make himself heard above the rising volume of noise from the riders who were now in distant sight. 'A lawman is a lawman or he isn't. If he tries to be anything else to accommodate people he has regard for, or who happen to be related to him, well . . . I don't think he's worth the weight of the tin in his badge!'

The sounds from the riders began to diminish, for as the

posse drew closer to the house, it slowed. And Strachen's voice was suddenly raised much higher than it needed to be to convey his opinions to Ruth and Adam Steele.

'All right, Marshal!' Gavin Fenton snarled suddenly. 'Get your prisoners ready to move out!'

There was a brutal harshness in his voice that caused the trio on the front lawn to snap their heads around and stare at the Broadwater sheriff.

They saw the glower Fenton directed back at Strachen bristled with a brand of hatred that had almost palpable force.

'What did I say?' the US marshal asked in a croaking whisper that carried only to Steele and Ruth as the dozen or so deputies reined their mounts to a dust-raising halt on the track at the side of the front yard.

Steele told him: 'You've seen the kind of town Broadwater is. You've worked with the sheriff. Fenton does the best he can. But to keep the job most men wouldn't do so well as him, he can't ever be so good at abiding by the letter of the law as you claim to be.'

'You mean——?' Strachen started, shocked.

'Nobody else's perfect, Albert,' Ruth cut in.

'Gavin Fenton is a crooked——' Strachen started to ask, ignoring his sister's remark.

But he was cut short again, this time by the violent interruption of a fusillade of gunshots. Then men yelled, dove to the ground from where they stood or as they got out of their saddles. Few of them could have realised for stretched seconds where the shooting was coming from through the drifting dust of the posse's halt.

Steele was first to recognise what was happening. Because as Strachen started to make the accusation against Gavin Fenton, he was looking at the Broadwater lawman, hoping for a reaction from him that might open the way for an escape bid.

But the bandaged head of Thomas Cramer showed in the doorway. And Fenton was given a shove in the back like the one Steele had given Ruth to plunge her into the house: to send him staggering out into the bright sunlight.

Then the gun that had accidentally killed Mathilde Cramer, been discarded on the floor and forgotten, began to spurt muzzle flashes and white smoke. And bullets.

135

Steele knew he made his move too late. For even as he crashed into the terrified Ruth, blood was already gushing from at least two bullet wounds in her chest.

When she fell, he went with her. First felt the rush of displaced air as a bullet missed his head by a fraction, then the scorch as one came close enough to graze the skin of his forearm.

He and Ruth hit the ground and he knew the sudden shudder that went through her meant she had just died in his arms.

She vented a soft sigh that he clearly heard against the tumult of screams, shrieks, curses and animal snorts that sounded after the gunshots ended.

But how could the woman have died in his arms? His wrists were shackled by the heavy chain of the manacles!

He cursed himself for being concerned with matters of no consequence as he felt a powerful surge of enormous grief overwhelm his emotions, threatening his sanity.

Then he snapped his head one way and the other. Desperately seeking a way to avenge the violent, undeserved death of the woman he loved.

But the scene suddenly darkened, as if in an instant the brilliant sun was obliterated behind a black cloud.

He wanted to scream his grief to the entire world, but he was struck dumb by an invisible stranglehold on his throat.

And he was abruptly deaf to the barrage of sound all around him.

But he clung to the presence of mind that enabled him to recognise it would serve no purpose to surrender to the temporary relief of passing madness. For that would allow others to dictate his part in the course of events which were now taking place in the wake of the tragedy that had hit him such a devastating blow.

Best to struggle to recall how he had once been able to harness the heat of anger, get it under tight, ice-cold control and use it to hone his reflexes while he fought back at the object of his rage.

He jerked his arm out from under Ruth's inert body. Saw that the wrist was free of the bracelet and knew this could not have been achieved by some superhuman feat of strength fueled by the degree of rage he had felt. Nor would Al Strachen have been negligent when he fastened the bracelet. So the manacles were faulty: had simply required a sudden jerk in a particular way to spring open the lock and free one of his arms.

And now the former restraints were transformed into a weapon: a length of flailing chain with the vicious weight of the open bracelet at the free end.

It had taken him less than a second to shake free of the threat of insanity that had confused his senses, and hone the anger. Required no longer than this to see what had happened and decide to capitalise on it.

Then it needed maybe a full second to power to his feet. Whirl and crouch. Identify the component parts of the scene.

He saw the group of newly arrived deputies were all still on the ground, starting to get up. They were yelling in confusion. Clawing out guns.

Al Strachen had his revolver drawn, aimed at the doorway, over Fenton sprawled face down on the lawn and struggling to push himself up on to hands and knees.

Behind Fenton, the grief-demented Thomas Cramer, the object of Steele's now tightly controlled rage, was on the threshold of the house. The bandage on his head and the fire scars marring one side of his face acted to emphasise his look of depthless despair.

But few were concerned with his expression, their gazes fixed on the gun in his hand that trailed smoke, just like after it went off and killed his wife, as it tracked this way and that. Never purposely aimed at anyone now it had ended the life of Mathilde Cramer's killer, but in turn momentarily menacing the deputies, Steele, Fenton and Strachen.

Steele lunged forward, his manacled wrists clutched in his free hand to increase the power to the swing of the flailing chain. And a roar of enraged intent burst out of his beard-fringed mouth.

There were shouts of warning.

Fenton powered into a roll out of his path, doubtless concerned the Virginian's attack was mindlessly directed at him.

Then there was a gunshot. And another: another. Holes showed in the broad chest of Thomas Cramer, spurted blood. The shot man tried to support himself with a hand on the

137

doorframe. Dropped the gun and used both hands. But then he died on his feet and toppled backwards, his legs kicked out across the threshold of the once carefully tended house.

Steele jolted to an abrupt halt. His suddenly impassive-eyed gaze shifting from the dead man to Gavin Fenton when the Broadwater sheriff said into the silence that followed the three shots.

'I'll kill you!'

He was sitting splay-legged on the grass, his Colt out and aimed at the Virginian. There was a look of horror on his square-shaped, heavily-lined face. His hat had been dislodged as he went down and the brilliant sunlight that fell unshaded across his features seemed to be dimmed by the fires in his eyes.

Strachen challenged in a croaking voice: 'He's my prisoner, Sheriff!'

The claim drew all attention to where he stood in the half crouch of an experienced gun-fighter, his left hand curled and still hovering over the revolver in his right from when he had fanned the hammer to blast the killing shots into Cramer.

'He was that one time before and you let him get away,' Fenton reminded coldly.

Steele lowered his arms, continued to clasp his right wrist in his left hand, the chain of the unfastened manacles hanging down in front of his legs to the lawn at his feet.

Strachen glared at him, seemingly intent upon snarling a warning at him. But he changed his mind when he saw Steele turn his head to look down over his shoulder at where Ruth lay on her side, one arm reaching forward, the other trapped under her unmoving, unfeeling body. The blood on the front of her dress bodice had already started to dry to an ugly brown colour in the high heat of the sun.

'Ruth's dead?' Strachen asked.

Steele was unable to offer a reply as he felt a stinging sensation in back of his eyes. He realised this was a threat of tears and while he fought to withhold them he knew it served to prevent him giving into a violent reaction to...

To what?

The man whose wife Ruth had accidentally killed had killed her. And now he was just as dead. Vengeance had been taken, then taken again. There was no one else left to punish.

Except Adam Steele himself, who was required to pay for killing Jim Bishop all those years ago. Years in which the heat of vengeance had been cooled. And now the cold and calculated due process of law could take its course. The law that cast such a long shadow through time and across space when a man as dedicated to duty as Marshal Albert Strachen was on the job.

'It was the way it had to be,' Strachen said without force.

But there was a coldness in his voice that drew Steele to look at him. The Virginian did not think the brother of the dead woman experienced a threat of tears and he accused:

'You're not even relieved you didn't have to kill her yourself, are you?'

Strachen looked at Steele, decided the Virginian was not going to try to use the shackles as a weapon again and thrust his gun back in the holster as he answered flatly: 'If it had been necessary, I would have.'

Fenton, back up on his feet, ordered the posse: 'Go get a wagon out of the Cramers' barn and hitch up a horse!'

All the men moved to complete the simple chore, bumping into each other in their hurry to be occupied.

'Like I said,' Strachen went on in the same monotone as he gazed down without blinking at Ruth's corpse, 'it would have made no difference she was my sister. The law's the law.'

'One good thing to come out of this,' Steele muttered bitterly.

Fenton snarled: 'Nothing good has happened here!'

The Virginian shook his head, growled: 'I reckon in this case I'd rather be an outlaw than his in-law.'

14

From a distance, it might have seemed as if the flatbed wagon the Cramers had used for hauling supplies from town and heavy loads around the farmstead was a hearse. And the driver and the riders grouped behind the rig were mourners at a funeral as they made slow progress along the track around the base of one of the highest hills on the western side of Lake Providence. Then turned on to the spur that skirted the northern end of the lake and joined the main trail into Broadwater.

Fenton drove the wagon with two of the Cramers' horses in the traces, the bodies of the married couple and Ruth Blair in the back, wrapped in individual bed blankets and covered by a single heavy tarpaulin, securely lashed down.

Steele, the ineffective manacles replaced by a length of firmly knotted lariat rope with much less slack between the wrists than the chain, rode immediately behind the wagon, astride the sheriff's gelding. He was hemmed in on three sides by the rest of the local lawmen and Al Strachen who was directly behind him.

Close up, there was little about the unshaven faces and dishevelled appearance of the group to suggest a funeral: unless the morose expressions of the men were seen as mournful.

Right after they started out from the Cramer place there was a low-toned exchange between two deputies that had caused a burst of laughter. Probably the humour was nothing more than a release of tension after the killings, but Fenton had put an angry stop to it: yelled at his men to have respect for the dead and sympathy for those who grieved for the dead.

After this, the mournful mood of some of the men became laced with disgruntlement, for few of them shared Fenton's sense of propriety and none felt personal loss because of the recent tragedies.

For a short while as the wagon creaked and hooves clopped at a funeral cadence, Steele was self-pityingly resentful that there was nobody around to give a damn about his condition: arrested for an ancient murder he might possibly hang for and grieving for the woman he loved, murdered just minutes go.

But this quickly passed. Along with the absence of talk.

Nobody spoke to him, but there was sporadic conversation around Steele as the men talked in soft tones in deference to Gavin Fenton's wishes. And for a time he made himself eavesdrop on what was said: on subjects that were the same as they would be any day anywhere a group of small town men were gathered together with time on their hands.

Women. Wives and children. The price of tobacco and liquor and beer. The job and its pay and conditions. The qualities of the latest guns compared with familiar old firearms.

He had no interest in anything that was said, but he did not listen because he thought he might overhear something of interest. It was just better to have his mind occupied rather than empty, when it was liable to drift and dwell in the depths of self pity.

In the end, though, the exercise was self-defeating. Since he found himself reminded of similar desultory talk he had overheard and sometimes engaged in on the infrequent occasions he had needed to kill time at the Golden Gate Saloon. Less often been coerced to attend a social at the Providence meeting hall.

At first he had always been something of an outsider, from choice as much as the attitudes of other people. But gradually as he became more firmly entrenched as a respected and even a well-liked resident to the area by his neighbours in the river valley and citizens of the town, he was encouraged to take a part in the talk and sometimes he did. Soon learned to enjoy being included in the exchanges.

So, as the wagon and the escorting riders rounded the northern end of the lake and he caught an occasional distant glimpse of Broadwater through the trees, Steele found himself again at the brink of the pit of misery from which he had endeavoured to draw back by not brooding on the death of Ruth Blair and how much he had lost by her violent passing.

For although the town beside the lake was not at all like

Providence in many ways, there were a great many ordinary, decent, law-abiding people who lived there . . .

'You say something, Mr Steele?'

He jerked his head up, turned toward the questioner. This was Luke Dexter, the deputy he had first had trouble with in Broadwater. After he had become a decent enough and ordinary enough member of the Providence River Valley community to lend a helping hand to a badly done by man and his two young daughters.

'What?' He had a vivid image of Esteban Garcia and Conchita and Maria as he looked at Luke Dexter.

'I thought you said something.' The deputy was abruptly apprehensive, like he was troubled by the look the Virginian gave him.

Steele answered with a brief smile he thought did not lighten the scowl in his coal black eyes: 'Maybe I did. But you have to make allowances.'

Dexter nodded, expressed something akin to sympathy as he said: 'Yeah, rough time.'

Then he looked pointedly away as he sensed the disapproval of his fellow lawmen: made it plain he did not want to talk about Steele's problems if that was what Steele wanted to discuss.

Steele faced front again, peered into the back of the flatbed and at the three clearly-defined humps contoured by the tarpaulin.

He knew which one was Ruth Blair only because he had seen the wagon loaded, the cover lashed into place.

The violent death of the woman was something he would regret for the rest of the life, no matter how long or short that turned out to be. He knew painfully little about her, but everything he did know he had found appealing. In hindsight, even her occasional childishness seemed attractive. And if there had been no one like her brother to show up and arrest him for Bish's murder, he might well have taken Ruth for his wife. By so doing, would have entrenched himself more firmly as a respected member of his community.

But that had not been the situation, damnit!

In terms of a US marshal coming to Trail's End to arrest him for murder, Ruth Blair whether alive or dead was irrelevant.

He would either have surrendered peaceably or attempted to avoid the consequences of the long ago killing. And there was little doubt he would have tried to escape. And, having successfully chosen that alternative in the circumstances that existed, Ruth had been an important consideration: one he would not have been without, knowing the kind of woman she was and how she felt about him.

But all else that happened might just as well have happened if he were on his own. Arrest, escape, flight, killings and recapture.

But that was all irrelevant, of course.

Ruth, who he had known and loved for just a few short hours, was dead and gone.

Trail's End, the place he had tended and nurtured over many years was equally beyond his reach in terms of ever running it again.

And if he should feel the need to reflect in misery on a painful loss, surely it should be the loss of Trail's End? For such could only be replaced once in a lifetime, if his experience of losing the Virginian plantation and finding a substitute in California were any yardstick. Particularly for a man on the run, wanted for murder.

Whereas women: they were thick on the ground, plentiful as fish in the sea, pebbles on the beach, stars in the night sky...

'Shit!' he heard himself rasp aloud this time. But he managed to stop himself voicing: '*Not the kind of woman she was.*'

'That's good, Steele, you oughta practise talkin' to yourself,' one of the deputies on the same side as Dexter growled harshly. 'In the event they don't string you up. Just lock you away in prison for a lot of years. Don't figure there'll be many guys of your style in there to talk to.'

Steele shifted his scowling gaze to the fat-faced man with sidewhiskers who was half grinning, half glowering at him. He vaguely remembered him as one of the posse halted on the track beside the front yard at the Cramer place, but could not recall him from Broadwater. But obviously he was a citizen of the town who knew the Virginian and had reason to hold a grudge against him.

'You're a great comfort in my time of trouble,' Steele muttered sardonically.

Then, paradoxically, felt a brand of gratitude toward the man. Who had his counterparts in Providence—and everywhere else. The kind who always had cause to be sour-tempered toward those who by hard work and tenacity laced with a little good luck achieved more than most. Steele was glad to be reminded that at the opposite end of the spectrum of human experience from depression and deprivation all was not sweetness and light.

'Don't pay any attention to Bernie,' Dexter growled. 'He's sore at you because he's the brother of Lonnie Crosby.'

'Uh?' Steele grunted.

'Guy whose nose you busted this morning when you crashed out of the Tivoli Hotel.

'Got somethin' to do with it!' Crosby allowed grimly. 'Mostly, it's because Steele killed a lawman way back. And whenever the sheriff deputises me, I'm a lawman and so——'

'Arguing back and forth is as bad as joking, you men!' Fenton snapped. 'Quit it!'

There followed another period of silence. During this, it was easy to imagine an almost audible grumbling of discontent trembling in the hot summer air as Bernie Crosby's friends sided tacitly with him against the others who did not share their dislike in principle for the prisoner. But the wishes of Gavin Fenton were adhered to and soon the wagon and its accompanying riders again became funereal in distant aspect.

In the malcontented silence, Steele found he did not have to force a thought process upon his mind to keep out unwanted notions. It seemed he had exhausted his capacity for experiencing self-pity over the material possessions he had lost and brooding regret for what might have been in a future with or without Ruth Blair.

They were gone and nothing could bring them back, so it did not matter. Thus he was now as he had been before Ruth Blair.

Before Trail's End.

If he chose, he could trace the start of the long shadow back to where it had its roots in Tennessee. To the moment after he let go the weighted corners of the thuggee scarf, knew Bish was dead.

It was a question of whether he was to be a prisoner or be free: if the worst happened, to be alive or dead. Which meant there was no doubt: no matter how bad life was, it sure beat being dead. However tenuous was freedom, it was better than being in the prison of which the surly Crosby had spoken.

So now his mind was spontaneously voided of all extraneous thought and he did not need to work consciously at keeping it this way, it remained blessedly blank. And he was able to concentrate on looking around, seeking a way to escape the fate that would be his if he remained a captive. Survey the wooded hills and lakeside terrain for an opportunity to cut and run: so long as the odds were in favour of survival.

And to hell with the consequences, even if it meant every man in this slow-moving procession of a wagon and horses perished in the process of achieving his end.

'Don't try it, Steele!' somebody warned from behind him.

He turned his head slowly to look over his shoulder, where he had not been directing his watchful gaze since he began to look for a way out of this. Because what was immediately behind him in the physical sense was as immaterial as the recent past. Nothing about the country in back of the slow-moving group could be of any service to him.

He saw Al Strachen was looking at him with bleak-eyed suspicion, a hand draped over the butt of the Colt which jutted out of his holster.

The marshal had spoken loudly and forcefully enough for his voice to cut across the clop of hooves and the rattles of the wagon and all heads turned toward him, the men expressing apprehension, expecting something to happen. Then they became intrigued when it seemed what Strachen had said was meaningless.

'What's the trouble?' Fenton asked grimly, like he thought the federal man might be trying to start some kind of less than reverential exchange of the type he had warned his deputies to avoid.

Strachen continued to gaze fixedly at Steele, then gave an almost imperceptible nod, acknowledging the Virginian had read what was in his mind. Steele had recognised he had seen, sensed or intuitively guessed with the experience of a skilled lawman that his prisoner had undergone a radical change.

'Steele isn't the same man he was at the start, Sheriff,' Strachen said.

'What?' Fenton sounded irritable.

'Be obliged if you'd instruct your men to watch him real close,' Strachen urged, carefully phrasing it as a request so he would not cut across the authority of the top man in whose jurisdiction he was working.

'What?' Fenton demanded again, looked around at the deputies as if seeking an explanation from them. Then he peered long and hard at Steele after the impassive-faced Virginian faced front again.

'Back at the farm, before my sister was killed, he agreed to surrender peaceably, Sheriff,' Strachen said. 'He even made a joke about needing arrest, if you recall?'

'So?'

'But he's changed now. I can sense it. Smell it, if you will.'

'Well, I tell you something, Marshall,' Crosby snarled as Fenton continued to gaze quizzically at Steele, but obviously learned nothing from the bearded face. 'I smell anything like a rat, I'll treat this guy like I would a rat in the basement.'

He curled a hand around the frame of the Winchester in his forward-hung boot.

Fenton directed a look of contempt at Crosby. Swept a less harsh gaze over his other deputies. Then hardened his eyes when they peered fixedly at the scowling face of Strachen as he accused: 'How can he try anything? He's tied up good and tight now and surrounded by more than a dozen armed men. Wearing badges that allow them to drop him like a mad dog—or a rat—if he tries to make a run for it!'

He started to turn toward the front again, paused to add menacingly: 'If I give the order to do just that!'

'And it sure will be a pleasure to follow that order, Steele,' Bernie Crosby muttered, a sneer spreading over his fleshy, side-whiskered, element-burnished face. 'So feel free to try somethin' uh?'

Steele drawled evenly: 'Sure would be a pleasure for me to feel free, feller.'

Strachen snarled: 'But he never will be. And he's the something that's going to be tried.'

Fenton took out his pipe and a poke of tobacco, growled: 'Just like my damn patience is being.'

They were waiting in the timber where the spur from the western side of Providence Lake joined the main trail north of Broadwater.

Steele saw the first sign of them first, because he alone was giving close attention to the terrain they were passing through, while with the exception of the pipe-smoking Gavin Fenton, everyone else was paying close attention to him: watching anxiously and eagerly for the trouble of which Al Strachen had warned.

Fenton had seemed withdrawn into a private world of deep thought after he lit his pipe. Peered constantly ahead, like he feared that to allow his gaze to drift to left and right or back over his shoulder would cause the wagon with its grisly cargo of corpses to run off the trail. Into the flanking timber, or the lake when the trail occasionally ran directly alongside it with no strip of gravel beach like that which fringed the water beside Front Street.

And it was at least a full second, maybe even more, after the first figure stepped out from the trees and on to the trail before Gavin Fenton vented an inarticulate sound with the tone of a curse, hauled on the reins and then cast a glance over his shoulder to snarl:

'No gunplay unless they——'

'Shit!' a deputy rasped.

'Will you look at that?' blurted another.

'How the hell did you fix this, Steele?' Strachen demanded.

Steele's only response was a slow shake of his head which he had already started before the marshal put the query to him. This as he took a tighter hold on the reins with his tied hands, ready to halt his horse as Fenton slowed the wagon.

It was the tall and lean, sixty years old Reverend Joseph

Marlow who first showed on the trail, attired in his full cleric's vestments despite the heat of the day close to noon.

Behind him came the thinner, almost as tall Lavinia Attwood. As always, she was primly dressed and had a cool, calm and collected look.

Then came the short and fat Ethan Brady, mopping with a handkerchief at real sweat on his face.

And behind the banker, the much more grossly overweight Thadius Mackay, his florid features as sweat-run as usual, no matter what the weather. His loud suit contrasted vividly with the sober hue of that of Brady.

Huey Attrill was next in the line, and although the side pockets of his stylish suit jacket bulged with notepaper, he did not actually have a sheaf and a pencil at the ready in his ink-stained hands. This, like the absence of a prayer book or a Bible in the grasp of the preacher, or the familiar black bag gripped by the doctor, indicated that the newspaperman was not here in his professional capacity.

Faith Kenway, renowned as the ugliest woman in Providence, followed Attrill into sight.

Then Harry Krim, the saloonkeeper.

Last of all, Clay Murchison, the crippled farmer from the south of town who had been so painfully involved in Steele's arrival in the Providence River Valley.

'Sheriff, I——' Strachen started.

'We don't know a thing until we hear them out!' Fenton cut in.

He took the pipe from between his teeth, knocked out the glowing embers and dead ashes against the side of the seat as he drove the horse to within twenty feet of the line of eight Providence people standing on the spur trail at the point where it joined the main one.

There was a short silence, uncomfortable rather than tense, after the wagon and horses were still. Everyone seemed reluctant to speak in the wake of the sheriff.

Steele felt the situation had suddenly become unreal, taken on the quality of a dream in which he had no part except as a detached observer.

Then Joseph Marlow stepped out from the line and moved into its centre. His tongue emerged to lick his lips beneath the pencil-line moustache, his deep-set eyes below their bushy brows blinking rapidly.

'Reverend?' Fenton asked, touched the brim of his Stetson. Added as he surveyed the array of some of Providence's most highly respected citizens: 'Ladies and gentlemen.'

'Sheriff,' Marlow countered.

'Friggin' polite, ain't it?' Paxton growled. The lack of reaction from any quarter meant his voice did not carry to Fenton and beyond to the Providence people.

'You must think there's something I can do for you?' Fenton asked.

'We'd like to know what is to happen to Mr Steele now that he has been captured, Sheriff.'

There was emphatic nods of agreement along the line of men and women with frowning faces. Just the two women craned their necks to seek out the Virginian behind the wagon, closely flanked by the lawmen.

'Me personally?' Fenton asked. This stirred up some discontented murmuring and an impatient shuffling of feet among the Providence people and he held up the hand clutching the pipe. He replaced this in a shirt pocket and said: 'Reverend, ladies and gentlemen. I've fulfilled my duty as sheriff of Broadwater. It's now up to the United States marshal to arrange for him to get to the county where he's wanted to stand trial.'

There was movement behind the wagon and Strachen rode his horse clear of the rest, to be plainly in sight, before he announced:

'I'm the US marshal.'

'Yeah, we heard that's what you were, Strachen. All the time you were actin' like you was somethin' else!' The broad-shouldered, pot-bellied, red-haired Harry Krim sounded brutally contemptuous.

Marlow looked uncomfortable.

Strachen remained calm as he pointed out officiously: 'I had a job to do. I still have it to do. And I should warn you people that any attempt to keep me from doing my sworn duty will——'

'We are not lawbreakers, sir!' Lavinia Attwood interrupted him indignantly.

'I should say we are *not*!' Faith Kenway agreed.

The widow storekeeper sounded and looked even more insulted than the spinster schoolteacher.

'Ladies, please!' Marlow entreated. He looked earnestly at them, accepted their compressed lips as a tacit sign they would remain silent from now on. Then he returned his attention to Strachen, explained: 'We would not contemplate any illegal action, sir. We came up from Providence only to ensure Mr Steele receives fair and just treatment.'

'After what we heard about you, we didn't trust a sneaky ba . . . guy like you to . . .' The owner of the Golden Gate Saloon let his voice trail away as he was given a withering glare by the Providence preacher.

Steele managed to say something around the unaccustomed lump in his throat and to his own ears his voice sounded normal when he asked: 'What did you people hear, how did you hear it?'

'You just keep it buttoned, mister!' Crosby ordered.

'Shut up, Bernie!' Fenton growled over his shoulder.

Strachen said before any of the Providence people could respond: 'I went to Providence before I came to Broadwater last night. I didn't know which direction you went and I put Sheriff Fallows in the picture. He figured you would try to lose yourself and Ruth in Broadwater for awhile.'

'Len is here with us in spirit, Adam,' Lavinia Attwood said.

Attrill added: 'But stickler for the law that he is, the sheriff didn't feel able to provide us with his physical presence.'

'What happened to Mrs Blair?' Marlow asked, and did an anxious double-take over the entire group in back of the wagon. His fellow citizens did likewise. 'The marshal's sister, I'm given to understand?'

'In the back of the wagon, preacherman,' Crosby growled.

'Along with a couple more dead bodies,' another deputy added callously.

Shock rippled along the line of men and women blocking the spur trail, and Ethan Brady asked in a shaking voice:

'You didn't . . .?'

He was looking at Steele, but it was Strachen who answered morosely.

'No, he didn't kill anyone today.'

150

The bearded Virginian told himself to be grateful his hands were tied. For had he been free, the way he felt at that moment he might have killed two deputies and even a banker.

Strachen went on: 'So Sheriff Fallows hasn't wasted time and energy like the rest of you by coming here. Sheriff Fenton, even Steele himself, will tell you: I'm a stickler for the law. And I can assure you I intend to see my prisoner gets safely to the appropriate authorities. Where he'll be given a full and fair trial.'

Krim muttered irritably under his breath. And the soured expression on the emaciated, pain-lined face of Murchison conveyed he was not entirely convinced by Strachen's claims. But the six members of the Providence deputation offered tacit acceptance of the premise with nods or by softening their scowls to frowns.

'Mr Steele?' Marlow asked.

'Reverend?' the Virginian answered the man who had always shown less regard for him than the other members of the group.

'We cannot, of course, help you out of your present difficulty. You must face up to the consequences of your actions in a court of law. But we feel—and a great many other people who know you share the view—that we are in your debt. For all you have done to help us in our times of trouble since you came to live among us. Times when all of us did not show our apprecia——'

'How long we gonna have to hang around here listenin' to this speechifyin'?' a deputy complained sourly.

'Yeah, how long?' Crosby agreed.

Strachen grunted in a way that did not imply disagreement with their views.

'For as long as the reverend needs to make his point,' Gavin Fenton said, then added: 'Long as it's not too long?'

Marlow shook his head, looked down at his empty hands like he suddenly missed having a Bible or some other religious text to occupy them. 'I'm almost through, gentlemen. Most of us know Steele is not a man of great sentiment, so I will not . . . But we know also he has a high regard for the home he has made for himself. A fine place that——'

Now Doc Mackay was suddenly as impatient as some of the lawmen for the exchange to end. He vigorously mopped at his cheeks and neck as he cut in: 'Want you to know, Steele. Long as we know there's a chance you'll be coming back to the valley we'll see to it your spread is taken care of. House kept locked up, stock tended, crops harvested, fence and buildings in good repair.'

'Grateful to you,' Steele said and this time his voice sounded to himself a little strained from the effort of trying to maintain an even tone. And, for the latest of many times, he was grateful the beard helped to mask any unbidden expression that might have crossed his face as he came to terms with the unexpected he found so difficult to handle.

'Len Fallows says the marshal convinced him real good you did what you're wanted for?' Clay Murchison growled miserably. He was once a policeman for the Southern Pacific Railroad, was wounded in the line of duty by a criminal.

'Right,' Steele said, glad the single word sufficed as a response.

'Damn!' Murchison growled.

'That's bad,' Brady moaned.

Faith Kenway shook her head sorrowfully and Miss Attwood suddenly did not look so cool and calm as she maybe fought back tears.

The rest of the group appeared disappointed by the easy admission of guilt.

'Does anyone now mind if I take my prisoner to where he's due?' Strachen asked, reproach mixed in with some triumph.

The Reverend Joseph Marlow looked over his shoulder in one direction and then the other. Drew nods from some of his fellow citizens and acquiescent expressions from the rest.

Crosby growled, his embittered voice barely audible: 'As if what they say or do makes any friggin' difference? They ain't got one gun between the whole bunch of them, that I can see.'

'Some people can make a forceful point without using force, Bernie,' Fenton murmured absently as Marlow ushered his fellow citizens off the spur.

But they did not go back into the timber from which they had emerged: instead started along the trail toward Broadwater, dragging their feet, morose expressions on their faces.

Some of the deputies looked grim, others resentful, a few

152

sullen: as was Strachen. But Steele felt suddenly exhilarated for a stretched second as he relished the unfamiliar experience of being respected by the majority of the citizens of Providence and the valley people.

'Pretty strange, uh?' Strachen asked, once more demonstrating a talent that approached mind-reading.

'Right,' Steele told him, again grateful a single syllable response was adequate for the purpose.

Fenton clamped his dead pipe between his teeth and started the wagon moving, into a turn on to the trail into Broadwater.

Strachen moved his horse back into the former position behind Steele astride the local sheriff's gelding.

The Providence people moved off the trail to the right, like they were clearing the way for the wagon and horsemen. But as the posse and its prisoner drew level, they could see into a small clearing where four saddlehorses and two buggies with animals in the traces had been left. One of the rigs was Doc Mackay's phaeton, the other the vehicle that Harlan Grout rented out.

'Something?' Fenton said as he once more halted the wagon, removed the pipe from between his teeth. 'Why'd you make your stand where you did?'

Murchison, crippled by rheumatism, and Mackay slowed by his obesity, were closest to the trail. While the others were already mounting up or climbing into the buggies.

'Wasn't no stand,' Murchison growled. 'We never could've been a match for——'

Mackay waved a hand at him in a quietening gesture. 'When we reached Broadwater and heard you'd gone around the lake, we planned to follow. But we saw you heading back this way. Since we didn't know if Steele would be brought back to Broadwater or Providence, or taken directly away by Marshal Strachen, the intersection of the trails seemed a good place.'

Fenton nodded and made a dismissive gesture with his pipe. Waited for the Providence people to move ahead along the trail to Broadwater, Mackay taking the reins of his own vehicle from Lavinia Attwood, Murchison riding with Faith Kenway in the rented buggy.

All of them directed sorrowful parting glances toward Steele, who called after them in a voice that still had to be forced out around the lump in his throat:

'I'm grateful to you. I'll see you get to know: one way or the other.'

'Only gonna be one way for you, mister,' Crosby growled.

'That's for a jury and a judge to decide, deputy!' Strachen snapped. 'In the fullness of time.'

'How much time, Marshal?' Fenton asked, not yet moving off in the wake of the Providence group.

'Uh?'

Fenton motioned with his pipe toward the departing people and the town to which they were heading, at present hidden by the intervening timber. 'I've got a jailhouse with plenty of room for your prisoner. But with that kind of feeling running for him, the faster you get him out of my neck of the woods, the happier I'll be. Preferably not on my horse?'

'Just what's left of the day to rest up,' Strachen answered. 'Come nightfall, we'll leave. Use his own wagon and horse to go north.'

'North?'

'San Francisco. There are two more marshals waiting there to assist with the escort duty. We plan to take him east by train.'

'Sounds fine to me,' Fenton said. And held back from setting the wagon rolling, to look long and hard at Steele. Then asked of the Virginian who was peering down the trail to where his fellow citizens had gone from sight around a curve:

'Surprises the hell out of me, Steele. Them folks going to all that trouble on account of you.'

'Yeah, it really tugs at the heart strings, don't it?' Crosby sneered with heavy sarcasm.

'I figure it'll make dyin' that much harder to do,' another deputy added, and Steele could not tell, nor did he care, if it was a sadly held opinion or a taunt.

'Quit it, you guys,' Luke Dexter said. 'Steele ever comes back here, you'll have cause to regret needling him like you're doing.'

'Come back?' Crosby challenged. 'The sonofabitch killed a lawman! He ain't got a ghost of a chance!'

Somebody giggled as the wagon and the saddlehorses started forward, then said: 'Could be that's how he'll come back, Bernie. To haunt you!'

16

For awhile it felt good to be alone in one of the six cells of the Broadwater jailhouse behind the Front Street law office.

He acknowledged to himself it would have been a whole lot better to be free, moving across open country and able to make plans for the new future that had been forced upon him. But in the present circumstances, this was not a bad place to be: locked in a cell with a barred window that looked across an alley to the blank side wall of a casino.

In the afternoon in this town that did not truly come alive until after dark, the gambling place was not doing any noisy business and because the alley was so narrow no shafts of hot, bright sunlight entered the cell.

There were no other inmates in the neighbouring cells, so he did not have to contend with any compulsive talkers or drunken snorers, which were the kind of prisoners so many western town jails seemed to hold.

The peace and coolness of the spartan cell, along with the relative comfort of the cot with its straw mattress, had much to do with his easy state of mind. But most of all, he could be philosophical about being locked up—and losing much more than his freedom—because of how the people of Providence had made their feelings for him known: and these just a small representative group of a much larger body of opinion, Joe Marlow had said.

But every now and then his contented mood was undermined by painful attacks of grief for Ruth, or embittered memories of Trail's End.

And then, as these emotions and a sense of guilt that he could experience any degree of easiness in such circumstances threatened to fire a futile anger in him, he was overcome by exhaustion: mental and physical. And suddenly, without any sensation of drifting from one state to another, he went from awareness to sleep: almost like he had been cracked over the head with something hard and heavy.

At the moment of waking he knew he had dreamed: was troubled by a vague memory of nightmare-like images competing for attention in his sleeping mind in a violent struggle that left his flesh run with sweat.

In the darkness that was just a little lighter than the pitch blackness behind his closed eyelids, he heard a confusion of distant sounds while in the law office a clock was chiming. He counted the notes to ten, but knew he might have missed one or two chimes before he woke.

Then his awareness was filled with the more raucous sounds from further away: the sounds of Broadwater at night—talk and laughter, music and clapping, shrieks and curses from the casino across the alley and other places along Front Street. Also, horses and wagons moving on the street which skirted the lake shore.

A moment later, there were footfalls within the building. A door opened and two figures moved from the law office into the jailhouse, one of them carrying a lamp.

'Steele, you awake?' Gavin Fenton asked.

'Yeah,' the Virginian answered as he sat up, swung his feet off the cot to the floor.

'You had more time to rest than we expected. Night fell a long time ago. It's midnight.'

He held the lamp, and had a key to open the cell door.

Strachen was beside him, running a length of rope from one hand to the other, like he was nervous.

The local sheriff said as he swung open the door: 'Brought in some food for you earlier. But you were so deep asleep, I figured you needed rest more than chow.'

Steele got to his feet. 'Be awhile before I need to eat that famous hearty meal, uh? That rope isn't long enough to hang me.'

'Got enough supplies to see us through to San Francisco without starving,' Strachen said. 'Are you back in a mood to come peaceably?'

Fenton held the lamp higher and draped his other hand over the butt of his holstered revolver. He stayed that way after

Steele had advanced on the doorway, thrust his hands out over the threshold so Strachen could re-tie his wrists.

'For now,' the Virginian said. 'But I'm making no promises for the future.'

'Wouldn't trust them if you did,' the marshal said.

In the lamplight Steele could see both men were freshly washed up and shaved. Gavin Fenton had even changed clothes for his evening duties, of which this was just one. He and his deputies always patrolled the streets of Broadwater at night: which was when trouble was most likely to break out in this town.

But, Steele saw as they went out of the building, unless Fenton had kept some of his part-time deputies sworn in since earlier, Broadwater's night life was having to look after itself for the time being. Because Luke Dexter, Ray Paxton, and the two other full-time deputies stood on the sidewalk, at the front of and in back of Steele's flatbed wagon with his gelding in the traces, directly outside the law office.

They were armed with holstered handguns and rifles held across their chests, not threatening the prisoner with anything except latent menace as they watched the street in both directions. At this end of town, Front Street was deserted. The door of the neighbouring gambling hall was firmly closed, doubtless by order of Fenton.

Steele recognised Strachen's mount hitched to the tailgate of the wagon, in the back of which was a heap of gear under a tarpaulin: maybe the same one that had been used to cover the bodies until they were delivered to Frank Chamber's funeral parlour.

'My rifle in back?' Steele asked.

'You ain't in no position to——' Ray Paxton started to remind sneeringly.

Strachen cut in: 'Yeah, and that fancy boot sheath along with the knife you carry in it. Everything else you own is at Trail's End still. And I'm not about to drive down there to get any of it.'

'Long as the rifle's aboard, feller.'

Nobody offered to help the Virginian get up on the passenger side of the seat. But with his hands tied in front, he was able to manage it with relative ease. Strachen climbed up beside him, took the reins and let off the brake lever, said to Fenton:

'You'll be sure to have Ruth's grave marked how I told the undertaker, Sheriff?'

'Sure, Marshal. And any time you're through here to look at it, or in the line of duty, you be sure to stop by and say hello.'

'I surely will.'

'You, too, Steele. If your luck gets better.'

'I'm grateful to you.'

The wagon started, the gelding in the traces eager for exercise after a day of rest in a local livery stable. Neither man looked back, nor said anything for a long time, while the wheels rattled and the timbers creaked beneath them. Then, when the town and its noise were far behind and they were moving through the dappled moonlight on the open trail in the timber, Steele asked:

'Is that why it took you so long to make the arrest, Strachen? You were waiting for help to reach San Francisco?'

'What?' He looked and sounded startled, like he was deep in thought and the sound of a voice jerked him violently out of his reflections.

'I'm not complaining, feller,' Steele told him. 'You did a good job of work for me all those weeks. And I had the extra time on the place. But after you tracked me to Trail's End, why did it take you so long to——'

'Yeah,' Strachen interrupted, and nodded. 'Well, it took me awhile to accept you were the man I was after. The name was right. So was the Virginian accent. And some of the stuff I started to hear about you in town fitted. Then some of it, along with what I knew about you ... Well, I figured I might need help to bring you all the way back east. So I telegraphed for some assistance.'

'From the Broadwater office?'

'Right. The reason I came to town those times. To send the telegraph and then to see if there was a reply. You know, it didn't surprise me too much: the way that bunch of people showed up, put in their two centsworth for you. Reason I never used the Providence telegraph office, I knew some people had a lot of respect for you.'

'Ruth showing up the way she did forced your hand, uh?'

'Yeah, it forced my hand. When I got back from Broadwater yesterday, I knew the extra marshals had reached Frisco. I'd wired them to wait there, because I knew you were fixing to go up there on business next week. Plan was to trail you up there, make the arrest in the city. But when I got back and found Ruth there, acting like you were everything her husband never had been, well, I——'

There was a gunshot. A rifle report so totally unexpected out of the dark forest that it was a sound that seemed to fill the world.

Strachen had said *I*.

Then came the shot.

Strachen made a soft, sighing sound against a series of fading echoes and then he was no longer seated beside Steele: was sprawled over the backrest of the seat.

And the horse, a little disturbed by the gunshot, came to a sudden halt as soon as the reins became slack.

Steele froze and felt utterly helpless as he considered the possibilities: rescue by one of a whole townful of people, or a ghastly mistake by somebody—Crosby maybe—gunning for him, who had aimed at the wrong man on the wagon seat.

There was no second shot. No sound from anywhere in the forest on all sides for long seconds that amassed until they formed into a minute.

Only then did he go through the motions of checking on the corpse of Al Strachen, just as he had made a cursory examination of the body of the hapless Matty Cramer in the parlour of the farmhouse on the other side of the distant lake. Saw the US marshal was as dead as any of those others who had died the day before this night, a hole oozing blood in the precise centre of his forehead.

Then, listening hard and constantly looking up from what he was doing, Steele climbed over the backrest of the seat into the rear of the wagon. Found his pitifully few belongings under the tarpaulin. First used the knife, the handle wedged between two warped boards of the wagon bed, to saw through the ropes which bound his wrists.

Nothing moved except for him and, every now and then, his horse. Or if it did, it made no sound.

When he was free, he retrieved the Colt Hartford, checked there was a live round in all six chambers of the cylinder and got down off the wagon. Canted the rifle to his shoulder and moved off along the trail: knew from the wound in Al Strachen's head that the shot had been fired from this direction.

Perhaps forty yards in front of where the horse stood silently in the tracks, his leading foot hit something on the trail. He was in a patch of deep moon shadow as he stopped, reached down and picked up what he had kicked. Experienced again the sensation of being in a waking dream as he recognised by feel what it was he was holding.

He carried it forward a few paces, into full moonlight: so he could clearly see he was holding a second Colt Hartford revolver action sporting rifle. Identical to the one he had inherited from his father which was canted to his shoulder. It even had an inscribed gold plate screwed to the side of the stock.

Then a familiar voice drawled from out of the timber: 'How're you doing, Reb? Not so good from what I saw, uh? But better, now you've got back . . .

. . . THE RIFLE.'●

●*This is the title of the next book in the Edge series.*